"We've got less than ten minutes. This time, I really do need you to hide. Will you do that? Please?"

"Tell me your plan first," she said, not answering his question.

"I don't have one," he said. "Other than to get more information out of them than they get from me and to keep you safe. Everything besides that is fluid."

She let out a loud breath.

"I can't focus on them if in the back of my mind, I'm wondering what you're doing," he said.

"Fine," she said. "I'll be in the back of the closet, hidden behind the clothes." She started to walk toward the bedroom.

"Stormy," he said.

She stopped. "Yes."

He put his hand on her shoulder, turned her and kissed her. All the emotion of the moment was packed into ten seconds of scorching pleasure.

Then he stepped back. "We're not finished," he said.

AGENT BRIDE

BEVERLY LONG

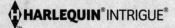
HARLEQUIN® INTRIGUE®

For Brynn and Eric, who both made the leap from college kid to adult look easy. Hope you're having fun in Missouri!

ISBN-13: 978-0-373-69875-2

Agent Bride

Copyright © 2015 by Beverly R. Long

Recycling programs for this product may not exist in your area.

This edition published by arrangement with Harlequin Books S.A.

For questions and comments about the quality of this book, please contact us at CustomerService@Harlequin.com.

® and TM are trademarks of Harlequin Enterprises Limited or its corporate affiliates. Trademarks indicated with ® are registered in the United States Patent and Trademark Office, the Canadian Intellectual Property Office and in other countries.

Printed in U.S.A.

www.Harlequin.com

Beverly Long enjoys the opportunity to write her own stories. She has both a bachelor's and a master's degree in business and more than twenty years of experience as a human resources director. She considers her books to be a great success if they compel the reader to stay up way past their bedtime. Beverly loves to hear from readers. Visit beverlylong.com, or like her at facebook.com/beverlylong.romance.

Books by Beverly Long

Harlequin Intrigue

Return to Ravesville

Hidden Witness
Agent Bride

The Men from Crow Hollow

Hunted
Stalked
Trapped

The Detectives

Deadly Force
Secure Location

Visit the Author Profile page at
Harlequin.com for more titles.

CAST OF CHARACTERS

Cal Hollister—After eight years, this former Navy SEAL is finally on his way back to Ravesville, Missouri. He's prepared to face a few of his own demons. But he's not prepared to find a beautiful woman, dressed only in a bridal gown, off the side of the road, half-frozen in an early winter snow.

Stormy—Cal dubs her Stormy, and she supposes it's as good a name as any. After all, she can't remember her own or how she came to be on the side of the road in a bridal gown. All she knows is that time is running out.

Pietro Moroque—When Cal and Stormy discover that he'd prepared the food for Stormy's wedding reception, they aren't sure whether they can trust him. On their first visit, he's reluctant to talk to Stormy. On their second visit, he's mysteriously missing.

Joe—He's a young, handsome bartender who knows Stormy. He's surprised by her appearance. Is it truly because he thought her work assignment had ended, or does he know something more about Stormy that he's not saying?

President LaTrope—He's the president of Moldaire College. He's invited his college fraternity brother, the Secretary of State, to be the honored guest at Saturday's football game. Is it possible that he did it with evil intent?

Mercedes Men—Four men intent on finding Stormy. The leader claims to be her cousin and that he's concerned because she has run away. Stormy might not know her own name but she knows none of these men are family and that if she ran from them, she had a good reason.

Chapter One

Cal Hollister rarely let anything stop him. And that included the weather. But when the freezing rain in the upper plains had turned to snow, then more snow, making the I-70 corridor a real mess, even he'd had to admit it was time to take a break.

Now, an hour east of Kansas City, Missouri, he'd filled up both his gas tank and his belly. He sat back in the tattered booth of Dawson's Diner and watched the television that was mounted in the corner of the truck stop. It was on mute and the words flashed across the screen. *Early winter storm paralyzes Midwest.*

Cal stopped reading, just as he'd turned off the radio in his rental car earlier. It was all they were talking about. The storm, the storm, the storm.

Missouri rarely got heavy snow and to get it in November was real news. He didn't care. He wasn't going to let a little ice and snow stop him.

He was going home. Back to Ravesville. The idea had taken root after Cal had talked to his brother last month and learned that Chase was getting the old house they'd inherited from their mother ready to sell.

Chase hadn't asked for help. He never did. Especially not from Cal. But it was time for that to change. Cal had finished his assignment and put plans in motion to get back to the States. It had taken a month but finally, he was a mere hundred miles northwest of his destination, more than three weeks early for Thanksgiving dinner.

"All finished?" the waitress asked as she passed the booth.

"That was amazing," Cal said. The woman had encouraged him to get the daily special, the roast pork, especially if he was pressed for time. He didn't have a schedule but he'd gone along with the suggestion.

She smiled. "I know. People are always surprised. They don't expect a place like this to have a chef. Pietro worked for years at Moldaire College in a high-end restaurant in their student union. He's always talking about how he used to cater all the important events at the college, even the private parties that the president of the college hosted." She picked up the dirty dishes. "Can I get you anything else? Maybe a piece of apple pie?"

"I'm stuffed but because I suspect it will be every bit as good as that roast pork, I'll take it to go."

"Good choice," she said. She walked over to the pie case, opened the door, slid a piece into a cardboard box, and brought it and a plastic fork back to the table.

Cal pulled out a twenty. "Keep the change, Lena," he said, looking at her name tag. She looked tired. Hell of a job slinging hash.

But at least she had a job.

Which was more than Cal had at the moment.

No job. No expectations to live up to. No one else's timetable to adhere to. It was a heady feeling for a man who'd spent eight years in Uncle Sam's employ as a Navy SEAL and the past six months as a contractor doing much the same kind of work at a considerably higher rate of pay.

"What are they saying about the roads?" he asked. He'd seen Lena chatting with two state police officers at the counter.

"It's bad and supposed to get a whole lot worse. Interstate is still open but there's lots of spinouts and cars in the ditch."

About what he'd expected. First bad storm always resulted in a bunch of fender benders as people relearned their winter math—that speed plus following too close equaled crap-on-a-stick.

He scooted to the end of the booth, stood up and stretched. "Well, wish me luck," he said.

She shook her head. "You're like all the other crazies around here today. There was a heck of a commotion in the parking lot right before you came in. People running around, slamming doors and carrying on. They cleared out fast when my friends at the counter, who never miss an opportunity for apple pie, pulled their squad cars into the lot. Probably couldn't wait to get out on the road and kill themselves."

That was a happy thought. He was grateful he'd missed the excitement. He'd had plenty recently. It had been less than two weeks ago that he'd barely missed getting up close and personal with enemy fire.

"Anyway, for what it's worth," she added, "there's a hotel about five miles east. They might still have a room."

He winked at her and smiled. Then he pulled his coat collar up and walked out the door. The cold wind hit him hard.

Crazy. Maybe. But Lena had no idea the number

of truly outrageous things he'd done. And usually in the name of protecting national security or preserving American interests.

The hotel might have been a good option if he was continuing on the Interstate. He would be turning off before that, for the final leg of his journey. The two-lane highway that would take him into Ravesville would likely be in worse shape than the Interstate but he had another hour of daylight left and he intended to make good use of that.

If everything went well, he'd be at the house in a couple hours. He thought about calling ahead but disregarded the idea. While Chase would intuitively know that the weather was a mere inconvenience to any former Navy SEAL, he still would worry.

Chase had always taken his big-brother role seriously. They were going to finally have a talk about that. The conversation Cal had been running from for years.

It took Cal ten minutes to brush the snow off his SUV. When he was finally back inside his rented Escalade, it was nice and warm. He pulled out of the parking lot.

The plows had gone through at some point but another couple inches had fallen after that. But he settled in, going a brisk thirty-five miles per hour. Two miles east, he took the exit, realized he'd been right that the secondary roads were in worse shape. It was somewhat reassuring to see wide tracks in the fresh snow. Somebody driving a big truck had made the same turn within the past ten minutes.

The wind was really whipping up the snow. It wasn't white-out conditions but damn close. Which was why he thought he was seeing things.

He checked his rearview mirror, didn't see any other cars and risked pulling over to the side. He got out, leaving his vehicle running.

Three feet off the road, something had hit the fresh snow, denting its whipped perfection. The object had rolled several more feet before stopping, forward progression halted by a study wooden fence that was likely there to keep cattle in.

He could hardly believe his eyes. There was a woman in a bridal gown and nothing else, no coat, no shoes, just a long veil, which was what had caught his attention. It was flapping in the breeze like a wayward flag.

She was on her side, turned away from him.

He figured she had to be dead.

SHE WAS SO COLD. Had never been so cold. And her head hurt. But she had to keep going. Had to get up. Get away.

She forced herself to move and heard a man swear. Suddenly there were hands on her. She had to fight.

No. No. She could not go back.

Felt a hand on her neck. She swung an arm, a leg. Knocked into something.

"Hey," he said. He pulled on her shoulder, flipping her to her back.

It hurt to open her eyes. The man was big and dark and he loomed over her.

She screamed and knew that no one was going to hear her. No one was going to help her. Just like before.

"How the hell did you get here?" he asked. But he didn't seem inclined to wait for an answer. She felt strong arms, one under her neck, the other under her knees, and she was swung up into the air.

He held her close, pulled tight against his coat.

And he started walking.

She tried to struggle, to force him to loosen his grip. But it was as if his arms were bands of iron. And her arms and legs felt heavy, useless.

She was dying. She knew it.

She closed her eyes and waited for it.

She felt him shift her weight. Suddenly, she was standing. She needed to run. Go. Now.

So tired.

Took one step. Saw the vehicle. Saw the door that he'd just opened.

"Get in," he said.

When she didn't move, he scooped her up again and deposited her into the warm, the heavenly warm, SUV. He shut the door. Within seconds he was climbing into the driver's side.

He was big and snow-covered and for one crazy minute, she could only think of the Abominable Snowman. But then he was moving, reaching a long arm into the backseat. She heard the sound of a zipper.

He had a big gray T-shirt in his hand. Suddenly, he was rubbing her face, her arms, brushing snow off. It was piling up on the floor, by her feet. He flipped the heater on high and more of the delicious heat poured from the vents.

His hands stilled suddenly. She looked down. He was staring at her left wrist. Saw his gaze move swiftly to her right arm. She looked, too. They matched. Both wrists sported a wide reddish band of skin.

And she remembered pulling, pulling with all her might. And being so angry.

"What happened here?" he asked, his words sharp.

She didn't answer. Just stared at him.

He hesitated, then reached into the backseat again. Pulled out another T-shirt, this one white and long-sleeved, and some gray sweatpants. "We've got to get you out of that wet dress," he said.

What?

She looked down. Saw what she was wearing and felt her heart start to race in her cold body.

How had this happened?

"Are you injured?" he asked.

Huh? He had evidently easily gotten past that she was wearing a wedding gown but she was having trouble moving on.

A wedding gown. She lifted her hand, touched the satin fabric, noting, rather dispassionately, that it was dirty in several places. Her hand started to tremble.

The man reached his own hand out, caught her fingers. "You're shaking," he said.

"Cold," she said. She had been. For sure. But that wasn't why she was shaking. Her body felt odd. As if she was on edge, just this close to spiraling out of control. At the same time, she felt nauseous, as if maybe she'd drunk too much and gotten too little sleep.

She turned her head to look at him. To try to offer up some sort of explanation.

"You're bleeding," he said, his cadence quick. "I didn't see that earlier." He leaned toward her and, with surprisingly gentle hands, prodded the right side of her head, just above her ear, with the tips of his fingers. She heard him hiss.

"You've got a hell of a knot here," he said. "But just a small slice in the skin. It's already stopped bleeding."

She reached up. Their hands connected and she

could feel his barely contained energy. His skin was warm. Vibrant.

He pulled his hand away. She continued to press and realized there was something on her head. A veil. Pinned tight into her hair.

She started yanking bobby pins and tossing them onto the floor. One bounced off the dash. She pulled and pulled. When the veil was loose, she ripped it off her head.

The man was staring at her, his hazel eyes assessing.

She reached up, pulled down the visor and stared into the mirror. Terror seized her, making her want to throw up.

Think. You need to think.

But it was as if all coherent thoughts had deserted her.

She started to shake. Badly. Not just her fingers or her hands. Her whole body.

And the man moved suddenly. Using both hands, he pulled the dry T-shirt over her head, stuffed both arms in. Pushed her forward in the seat, so that he could reach around her back. She felt him release the zipper of the dress. Felt him unclasp her bra.

Then he was pulling down her dress, her strapless bra, and lowering the T-shirt at the same time, preserving her modesty. His touch was quick, impersonal, but she felt the intimacy of it. She shook his hands off.

If she didn't do this, he would.

She pulled the T-shirt down. It came to her thighs. Then she yanked on the wet, heavy wedding dress. When she had it off, she handed it to him. He tossed it into the backseat. She pulled on the sweatpants, cinching the tie strings as tight as she could. When he handed her thick white socks, she put those on, too. She was drowning in his clothes but it felt absolutely wonderful to be warm and dry.

"I'm not sure where the nearest hospital is," he said, "but I think our safest bet is to head back to the Interstate."

Hospital? She grabbed his arm. "No."

He stared at her. "What the hell is going on here?"

She had no idea. All she knew was that she couldn't go to a hospital. Couldn't go anywhere.

They would find her.

"What's your name?" he asked.

She didn't answer. Couldn't trust this man with the truth.

He waited.

"What's your name?" he asked again.

"Mary. Mary Smith."

He narrowed his eyes at her. "I don't think so."

She said nothing.

"How about I just call you…" He paused. Then looked forward, into the blowing snow. "Stormy," he finished. "That'll do."

"What's your name?" she asked quickly, desperately trying to shift his focus.

He seemed to hesitate for just a moment. "Cal. Cal Hollister." He put the car in gear, pulled back onto the highway and started driving.

"Where are we going?"

He didn't answer her.

He was taking her to the hospital. She just knew it. She had to get away. She reached for the door latch.

He was faster, stretching his arm across her body, blocking her hand. "Please. I would like to help you.

I just came from a diner where there were two cops. I think they may be your best bet."

The police. Again, she could feel her heart start to race. Why? She searched her mind, her terrifyingly empty mind, and tried to reason it out. Was she in trouble with the police? Was she running from the police?

"I just need a place to stay. To get some sleep," she said. "Can you just drop me off at a hotel?"

He waved his hand in a semicircle. "We're sort of in the middle of nowhere."

She could see that. Everywhere she looked there was snow. And it was getting dark.

"Will you drive me as far as the nearest town?" she asked. "I'll pay you. I promise. I mean, I don't have any money with me, but I'll send it. Just give me your address."

He stared at her, his eyes showing absolutely nothing. Was he about to kick her out of his car, thinking that she was going to be more trouble than she was worth?

"I won't be any inconvenience," she promised.

"There have to be people looking for you, worried about you. At the risk of stating the obvious, I think today might have been a big day for you."

Had she gotten married today?

She didn't think so. She'd know that. Deep down she would know. Right?

"I'll contact people once I get to the hotel," she said.

He reached into his pocket and pulled out a cell phone. Handed it to her.

Her arm felt as if it weighed eighty pounds when she reached to take it. Her fingers brushed against his.

Warm skin.

So different.

And a flash of a memory, jagged at the edges, in grays and blacks, like an old movie, jumped into her empty head. Cold hands. Wrapped around her upper arms. Pushing her. Cold, cold hands.

She closed her eyes. Willed it to come. But that was it.

"Please just take me to the nearest hotel." She put his phone down on the gearshift console. Maybe rest would help.

If it didn't, she didn't know what she was going to do.

Chapter Two

Under normal conditions, having a beautiful woman beg him to take her to a hotel was not an invitation that he needed to give much consideration to.

Hell, yes.

And if all went well, a half hour after they'd checked in, neither one of them would even remember it was snowing.

But there was nothing normal about this. The woman had been lying in the snow in a wedding dress. As he'd approached, he'd seen a slight movement in her arms and legs and had reached out to check for a pulse. She'd responded like a mad dog, throwing a punch and kicking her leg. Her movements had been uncoordinated, as if hypothermia was setting in.

While he had no formal medical training, every SEAL had the basics. He'd quickly sorted through the options. Moving someone before a full assessment was always a risk. But her extremities all seemed to be in working order, maybe a little jerky, a little awkward. He'd identified the cold as his biggest challenge, decided there was no time to waste and flipped her over to her back.

Then, even though her arm and leg hadn't connected

with anything vital, he'd been knocked back and just a little breathless.

She had a stunningly beautiful face. Dark hair. Very dark eyes, almost black. Rich, almond skin that hinted at an ethnicity that was more exotic than his own common German-Irish mix. Maybe from one of the Pacific Islands.

When she'd screamed, he'd gathered his lust-spiked wits and moved into action. He didn't think she'd been there long. Dressed as she was, it would have taken less than twenty minutes in these conditions—twenty-degree temps with a thirty-mile-an-hour wind—for her to be in real serious trouble.

He hadn't been confident that she could walk, so he'd carried her to the car. Once inside the vehicle, he'd been processing what to do next when he'd seen the marks around her wrists that looked suspiciously as if she'd been tied up.

It was possible that it had been consensual. What people did behind bedroom doors was nobody's business. But he'd spent the better part of the past decade in countries where men routinely mistreated women and he couldn't get the idea out of his mind. But when he'd asked, she'd stared at her wrists, as if it was the first time that she'd seen them, seen the damage.

Then he'd seen the small trickle of blood on the side of her face. He'd been very concerned when he'd felt the lump on her head, which he suspected she'd gotten from connecting with the fence post, and had been relieved when he'd seen that the cut itself was just a slice that would heal quickly.

He'd pushed aside his concern over her possible

mistreatment and dealt with the immediate need of getting her out of her wet clothes.

When he'd pulled the T-shirt over her head and lowered her dress, he'd done a quick inspection of the rest of her to assess for injuries. Had caught a glimpse of pretty breasts and smooth skin but no other significant bruises or red marks.

The wedding dress had been wet and heavy and, quite frankly, had knocked him off his stride.

And oddly enough, it had seemed to have a similar effect on her. She'd ripped the pins out of her veil as if she was attacking a nest of snakes with a garden hoe. Her wet dark hair, free of constraints, had fallen around her shoulders.

How had a bride ended up in the snowdrift? Where the hell was her husband?

When he'd picked her up, he'd made a visual inspection of the surrounding area. No footprints besides the ones he'd left. No sign of a vehicle, with the exception of the wide tire tracks on the road, but he was fairly confident that the truck hadn't stopped. There was no sign of heavy exhaust in the fresh snow that would have been there if a big truck had idled for any amount of time.

Was it possible that she'd fallen out of the truck while it was moving? That someone had pushed her out?

None of it made sense and she wasn't helping. She'd lied about her name. He was pretty sure about that. Had tried to let her know that he knew in a nice way by calling her Stormy instead. When she'd asked his name, he could have reciprocated and lied. He had a half-dozen different aliases that he'd gone by in the past years. Instead, he'd offered up the truth.

It might have been a mistake but he'd felt the need

that one of them should be honest. Why it was important, he wasn't sure. They were ships passing in a storm. He was offering a helping hand until she could reach out to someone else.

Which she didn't seem inclined to do. He'd expected her to look upon his cell phone as an unexpected lifeline but there didn't seem to be anybody she was interested in calling.

Odd. To say the least.

There were probably a couple choices. He could keep driving toward Ravesville and take her to the old house. But given that he didn't know her story, he wasn't inclined to want to do that. It was too great of a risk that he might be bringing trouble to his family, to Chase especially, and he was done with that.

He had enough guilt already.

He could disregard her instructions that she didn't need either a hospital or the police and drop her off at whichever he encountered first.

Or he could turn around, take her back to the Interstate, find the hotel that the waitress had said was just miles down the road and send her on her way.

That was probably the best option. Now that he'd gotten a closer look at her, he could see the fatigue that shadowed her eyes. He supposed it was a busy time leading up to a wedding.

Had she gotten cold feet? Was there a groom pacing the aisle in some church, at a loss to understand where his bride might be?

But it was a Tuesday. Cal didn't know much about weddings but he was fairly confident that they were usually on a Saturday. Maybe she was simply unconventional. Maybe she and/or the groom worked on the weekends. Maybe they got a better price on the reception if the event was on a weekday. Could be a hundred explanations.

She did not, however, look interested in offering up any of them. She was staring straight ahead, her arms wrapped around herself.

In all likelihood, he'd saved her life. It would be nice to know her name but not necessary. He wasn't the type to brag or dwell on past accomplishments and this, quite frankly, wasn't the first time he'd saved an unknown person's life. That was what SEALs did best. Save the good guys. Kill the bad guys.

He was going with the assumption that she was on the side of right and that he wasn't assisting the wrong person. That was what his gut told him and he'd learned to listen to it.

"Buckle your seat belt," he said. He checked his mirrors, slowed down and then made a narrow U-turn on the snow-covered highway.

"Where are we going?" she asked, her voice small.

"Back to the Interstate. There's a hotel a couple miles east. I'll drop you off there."

He turned on the radio. Maybe he'd try to get some information on the weather after all. It seemed as if the storm was picking up in intensity. It dawned on him that he hadn't cared as much when he'd only had himself to worry about. Now he was responsible for her.

It should have felt suffocating to a man who'd recently deliberately shed all his formal responsibilities. At least irritating that he'd been sucked back in so quickly.

But oddly enough, it felt okay.

"Don't worry," he said.

She said nothing for a long minute. Over the sound of the radio, he could hear the tires working hard to grab pavement.

Finally she turned to him. "Thank you," she said. "I owe you."

IT WAS TRUE. She owed this man her life. But as soon as she could, she was getting away from him. He was young, maybe not even thirty, but his hazel eyes seemed to hold knowledge beyond that. He had short dark brown hair in a buzz cut and his skin was very tanned.

The only time he'd really pushed for information had been when he'd asked her name. She'd had to tell him something. And he'd called her on the fact that he didn't think it was legitimate. Yet he was still willing to help her.

She wished she could accept that it was as simple as one human being extending a kindness to another. But something told her that she should trust no one. *No one.*

He was a good driver. His hands were relaxed on the steering wheel. She'd have been a nervous wreck.

She didn't like to drive in bad weather.

Didn't know how she knew this. Just knew it.

In less than five minutes, they were on the Interstate that he'd mentioned. She saw a sign. St. Louis, 194 miles.

St. Louis. She let that dance around in her head for a minute. "Joe Medwick. Ducky Medwick," she corrected.

He turned to stare at her. "What?"

"St. Louis Cardinals. He holds the record for most runs batted in during a single season. Late 1930s."

"Thirty-seven," he said, "1937." He paused, then added, "How the hell did you know that?"

She'd surprised him. Oddly enough, that made her want to smile. Nothing else that had happened up to this point had seemed to faze him but he looked absolutely flabbergasted that she knew baseball. "Sports trivia is not reserved for the male species," she said.

"Right," he said. He was silent for a long minute. "Motel should be just up the road." He paused again. "Have you eaten lately?"

She didn't feel hungry. "A little while ago," she said.

He nodded and kept driving. The SUV churned through the snow on the road, its tires slipping occasionally as they encountered patches of ice. They stayed on the road, however, which was more than she could say for the three cars they passed that were in the ditch.

It took them fifteen minutes to get to the hotel. He pulled into the lot and she stared at the building, trying to catch some feel for whether she'd ever been here before. She didn't think so.

It was a two-story wood building, painted mostly red with some white trim, with each room having an exterior door. She counted them. Eight up, eight down, with a small office at the front of the building. The parking lot was full of cars and had already been plowed at least once. There was a big white sign with blue lettering and a red border. The Daly American Inn. There was a flagpole and a flag near the front door. She wondered if someone had braved the elements that morning or perhaps they simply never took it down.

She stared at the flag, watched it flap in the wind, partially obscured by the flying snow. Something fluttered in her chest. "Oh," she said, putting a hand to her heart.

"Problem?" he asked.

She shook her head. What could she say? *Yes, plural but none that I can talk about.*

He took the space in front of the office. She gripped the door handle tight. "Like I said, I don't have any money on me."

He shrugged. "We'll worry about that once we know if they have a room. I'll go check."

It sounded as if he was willing to pay for it. Thank goodness. She would send him a check. Right away. She paid her debts. At least she thought she did.

He got out of the vehicle and snow blew in. It was really getting cold.

She watched him walk into the office. His dark down jacket came only to his waist. He wore jeans and cowboy boots and with his narrow hips and nice long legs, he was totally rocking the look.

It felt a little ridiculous that given the circumstances she had even noticed. But it was also oddly comforting, as if her subconscious was letting her know that everyday pleasures, even those as basic as admiring a sexy stride and a fine rear end, were not beyond her grasp.

The office was well lit and she could see a young man behind the desk. He was staring down at his cell phone, punching buttons. He looked up, evidently listening to whatever Cal was saying, and shook his head.

Her heart sank. She hadn't realized how much hope she'd had pinned on getting a room, having a place to rest. If that wasn't possible, she had no idea what she was going to do. Maybe they would at least let her sit in the office until…

Until what?

That was the great unknown.

She saw Cal reach into his pocket. Push something across the counter. Take the plastic key that the young man offered.

Hallelujah, it looked as if it was going to be okay.

When Cal returned to the vehicle, he handed her the plastic key. "You got the last room," he said.

"I was worried. I saw the clerk shaking his head."

"Just didn't understand what I was asking for."

It was perfect. She could sleep. For as long as it took. Then wake up and be able to deal with everything.

"How much do I owe you?" she asked. "I want to keep track."

"Rooms are eighty-nine bucks a night. You're in number fourteen. Second floor, two doors from the end."

"Perfect."

"How's the head?" he asked.

"Still hurts," she said honestly.

"Nauseous?" he asked.

She actually felt better than she had a half hour earlier. "No."

"Your pupils look normal," he said. "Which hopefully means that you don't have a concussion. But I'm still worried about that. You're sure that you're going to be able to call someone to help you?"

"Absolutely," she lied.

He drove the SUV to the corner of the building where her room was located and put the car in Park. He reached into the backseat and pulled out another pair of thick white socks. "Your feet are going to get wet walking in. Take these so you have something dry to change into."

He was a really nice guy. "Can I have your address?" she asked. "To mail you a check. For the hotel, and these," she said, waving at the clothes he'd given her.

He shook his head. "Don't worry about it. Pay it forward someday."

That was a nice idea. "Well," she said. It was crazy but she didn't like the idea of getting out of the car. She felt as if something bad was about to happen. But this man had done enough for her. There was nothing to be gained from stalling.

"Thank you," she said. She extended her hand.

There was a slight pause before he reached out and very formally shook her hand. His index finger had a callus and she resisted the urge to rub the pad of her thumb against it. "Good luck," he said.

She swallowed hard. Some good luck would be nice. She opened the door and got out. She went to close the door.

"Hey," he said. He pointed to the backseat. "Don't forget this."

Her wedding dress. She grabbed it and the horrible veil that had hurt her head and wadded them under her arm. She ran up the exterior staircase and inserted her key into the door. It opened. She turned.

He was still there. Watching.

She waved.

He nodded and pulled out of the parking spot.

She went inside, feeling strangely sad. She should be happy to be free of the man. She needed time to figure out what to do next and she needed to be totally focused. That would have been difficult if Cal Hollister had stuck around.

She sat down on the ugly green-and-gold bedspread
and stared at the tan carpet. What the hell was she going
to do?

CAL'S FRONT FENDER was edging out of the lot when he
decided that he might be a fool but he didn't intend to
be a hungry one. He still had the pie that he'd tossed
into his backseat but it wouldn't hurt to have a backup
supply of candy bars, chips and red licorice, his favorite, if he did happen to get stuck. And the hotel vending machine was probably his best bet.

He backed up, parked his SUV and went inside. The
desk clerk, phone still in hand, looked up. Cal waved at
him and pointed his index finger at the vending machine
in the alcove off to the side. The kid smiled back. When
Cal saw the prices, he realized the kid was probably
laughing *at* him, not with him. It was practically highway robbery. But he started feeding in his dollar bills.

Stormy had seemed a little reluctant to get out of
the car. And he'd had the craziest urge to want to keep
talking to her. Maybe they could have traded baseball
trivia. She'd surprised him with that one. Her eyes had
lit up and he'd gotten a glimpse of what her face would
look like without fatigue and cold clouding it.

He'd felt an attraction to her. And that, ultimately,
had been what had kept him from chatting it up in the
car. She was either someone's fiancé or someone's wife.
Off-limits.

Just two years ago, he'd had to pick up the pieces
when his best friend on the team had gotten a Dear
Leo letter. Leo's wife had met someone and had filed
divorce papers. Leo had gone a little crazy and Cal had

been seriously worried that the man was going to make a mistake that could take the whole team down.

He didn't ever want to be in the middle of something like that. So he'd said goodbye to Stormy and accepted that how she came to be in that snowdrift, in her wedding gown, was going to be one of life's unanswered mysteries. When he'd checked in, he'd verified that there were phones in the room. Hopefully, by now she'd made her calls and help was either on the way or, at the very least, relieved to hear that she was okay.

He had just pressed the last button when the door opened. Two men, both wearing long black coats and dark pants, came in. The taller man had an ugly scar, running from the corner of his eye to halfway down his cheek.

Both men gave Cal a cursory look but focused on the desk clerk. "We are looking for our cousin," the taller one said. His tone was low, almost guttural, and he'd turned his back to Cal. But Cal, who had always had excellent hearing, didn't have any trouble making out the words. The guy had a slight accent, clipping the end of his words, rolling his *r*'s just a little. Maybe Russian.

The man held out his smartphone so that the clerk could see something on the screen.

"Pretty bride," the clerk said.

"Yes, very beautiful," the tall man said. "Have you seen her?"

Cal casually reached into his pocket and fed in another dollar. Took his time considering his choices.

"Nope," said the clerk. "I'd have remembered her if she'd checked in," he added with the exuberance of a horny young male.

The two men looked at each other. They were frustrated. Trying to hide it but not doing a great job.

"It is very important that we find her," said the shorter one. "She would have arrived within the last hour."

The desk clerk nodded. "Sorry I can't help. I'm the only one here. If she'd have rented a room, I'd know it. There are a couple motels down the road another ten or fifteen miles. You may want to try there."

The two men nodded and walked out the door. The shorter one had a stiff left leg, swinging it from the hip, rather than bending it at the knee. Cal grabbed his purchases and stepped back into the main office. Glanced out the window. They were driving a black Mercedes. They pulled out, headed east.

Cal held up his bag of chips. "My favorite," he said. "Should get me through the night."

The clerk shrugged and picked up his phone.

Cal pulled up the collar of his coat, opened the door and walked back to his vehicle. Once inside, he started it and flipped on the wipers to clear the windshield of snow.

Pretty bride.

Very beautiful.

Arrived within the last hour.

One only had to be smarter than the average bear to figure out that they were talking about Stormy, or whatever her real name was. And they seemed pretty determined to find her. Cal figured they'd be back for a second check once they got up the road a ways and nobody had seen her.

Really wasn't his problem.

He glanced in his mirror and sedately pulled out of the lot.

Chapter Three

She took a shower and stood under the hot spray for a long time. She stared at her wrists, rubbed them with the washcloth, noting that they were tender. Bruised.

She shampooed her hair, carefully rubbing the bump and the open cut. It stung a little but she figured that was a good thing. Even though it was just a small cut, it was probably a good idea to get it cleaned out.

Not that getting an infection was her biggest problem.

She got out of the shower, dried off and used the small bottle of lotion provided by the hotel. She rubbed Mango Magic on her legs, her arms, her hands. She thought her knuckles were chapped from her time in the snow but realized that they were skinned up and several of her nails had broken off, leaving a jagged edge behind.

She had a very vague recollection of grasping something with her hands, slipping off, grasping again. Hanging on.

She could feel her anxiety mounting and she told herself to breathe deep, to not try to force it. She towel-dried her hair, wishing she had a comb. At least the hotel had provided a blow-dryer. She used it, running her fingers through her hair, jerking when one of her jagged nails caught a strand and pulled.

She used her finger along with some soap to *brush* her teeth. Then she rinsed and rinsed, feeling as if had been days since her teeth had been clean.

She opened the bathroom and was very grateful that she had a towel wrapped around her because Cal Hollister was sitting on her bed, back propped against the headboard, arms behind his head.

He was chewing on a stick of red licorice.

What the hell? "Get off my bed," she said, working hard to keep her tone even. She would not let him see that she was scared to death.

"No." He reached down to the end of the bed, where she'd left his T-shirt, sweatpants and her underwear. He scooped them up and tossed them in her direction.

She reached automatically and almost lost her towel in the process.

"Get dressed," he said.

She stepped back inside the bathroom and slammed the door. Looked for a lock but there wasn't one. Of all the nerve. He may have saved her life but who did he think he was coming here, surprising her, putting her at a disadvantage? She yanked on her clothes, grateful that she'd put the strapless bra in the pile, along with her panties. Once she was finished, she looked around the small room for a weapon. Saw the only thing that might work. A minute later, she walked out, her hands together, casually cupped at her belly button.

She crossed in front of him, sat in the chair near the door. His duffel bag was on the floor, near her feet. From this angle she could see that he had an assortment of candy bars and chips on the bed next to him. "Going for a sugar high?" she asked.

"Always." He tossed her a Hershey's candy bar. She let it fall in her lap.

"Got these from the vending machine in the office," he said.

She waited. Where was this going?

"While I was there, two men came in. Squirrelly-looking guys. Lots of black hair and gold jewelry. One guy has a big scar on his face. Other one had a bad knee."

He was watching her. "Okay," she said.

"They showed the desk clerk a picture of someone on their phone. Someone, according to the clerk, who was a pretty bride."

She could feel her stomach clench. "What did the clerk say?"

"Said he didn't have anybody here that resembled the woman."

She felt some of the pressure lift off her chest. "They left?"

He nodded. "I suspect they'll be back. Them and their friends."

"Friends?"

"The first two left in a black Mercedes but there was a matching vehicle parked toward the back of the lot. It stuck around. I suspect they were waiting to see if the clerk was lying. If he was, it would be a fairly safe assumption that he'd make a mad dash to the person's room or use his cell phone that appears attached to his hand to put out a warning call. They might have been expecting somebody to quickly exit from one of the rooms."

"But that didn't happen," she said.

"Nope."

"Did the two men see you?"

"Yes. So I suspect the guys in the second car were also told to watch me. So I drove off, in the opposite direction of the first car. I waited to see if they'd follow me. But they didn't. They went the same direction as the first car. Probably didn't want to get split up in this weather."

"But you came back?" Why? To warn her? Or maybe he'd decided that there might be a way to profit from this unexpected encounter. Maybe he'd considered whether the men might be willing to pay for information on her. "How did you get in?" she asked, feeling very vulnerable.

He held up a plastic key card. "When I first checked in, I asked for two rooms. I thought maybe I'd try to get some sleep before going on to my final destination. That's when the guy told me that he only had one room with one bed. I told him that I'd take it, that my brother and I would have to sleep together. I laughed it off, said we'd done it as kids, that we could probably do it for one more night. He gave me two keys, one for me and one for my brother."

She'd seen the hotel clerk shake his head. When she'd asked Cal about it, he'd dismissed it. *Just didn't understand what I was asking for.*

"You lied to me earlier," she said.

He shrugged. "I thought if you knew that I was interested in getting a room that you'd feel compelled to offer to share this one. I didn't think that would work out so well for you when your new husband showed up."

She did not have a new husband. At least she didn't think so.

"You might want to take your wedding gown and veil out of the garbage," he said, looking in the far corner. "That might not make him feel so great, either."

She'd stuffed the offensive items into the brown plastic wastebasket. They spilled over the edge.

"You know," he said, "that's how I found you. I saw your veil blowing in the wind."

It was a miracle that he'd been able to see it, especially in white-out conditions. Most people would have driven by, clueless that a woman was freezing to death.

She was getting a sense that Cal Hollister wasn't *most people.* "So the hotel clerk thinks there are two men in this room. He doesn't know about me," she said.

"Nope. I suppose it's possible that he saw you get out of the car but I don't think so. Angle was wrong, plus the guy is obsessed with whatever he has on his phone."

She was safe. For the meantime. But who were these men? Why would they be chasing after her? She lifted her chin. "I certainly appreciate you letting me know," she said.

He sat up and frowned at her. "Congrats on being so very civilized and proper. Here's the thing, though. I don't think they were here to invite you to tea. So, I don't think good manners are going to be all that helpful in this situation."

He wouldn't think she had a civilized bone in her body if he knew how close she was to losing it, to screaming and kicking the damn bed.

"Why are they looking for you?" he asked.

"I don't know."

"Come on, Stormy. You can do better than that."

"I. Don't. Know. And I don't know who the men are. In fact, how do I even know that you're telling the truth?" She tossed her hair and tried not to wince when it hurt her head. "How do I know that you didn't just want a reason to come back to my room? How do I know that you're not my biggest worry?"

He stood up. "If I was, you'd already know it for sure. Now, I suggest you start thinking about what you're going to do when those men come back. I know the type. They won't want to be bested by a woman. And whoever is paying for those expensive cars isn't going to be happy that his guys couldn't get the job done. When they don't find you up the road, they'll come back and start turning over rocks. The motel clerk will break in about ten seconds and he'll be opening every one of the rooms for them to inspect."

Something told her that he was right. Some past experience.

"How long do you think I have?" she asked.

He shrugged. "They told the desk clerk that you would have arrived within the last hour. So, I think their radius will be anywhere you could have gotten in an hour. On a normal day, that's seventy miles, give or take. Today, half that at most. Today, they'll be forced to stick to the main roads. But in a day or less, when this storm dies down, they'll be able to cover ground much more quickly."

"How long?" she repeated.

"I think you've got eighteen to twenty-four hours. After that, you better be on your game."

Was she on her game? Not hardly. Something flashed in her head. She shook it, trying to clear it.

"What?" he prodded, maybe thinking that she wasn't taking the threat seriously.

"You said I needed to be on my game. And all I can think of is Leon Durham."

"The baseball player?" he asked, as if he really couldn't believe it.

"Yeah. He played first base. Talented player but unfortunately, there was the time he let a ball roll through his legs."

"In 1984. Cubs versus Padres," he said. "Padres went on to win." He paused. "How the hell do you know these things?"

She had no idea. It was just there.

It was horribly frightening. She had men chasing after her and all she had a grasp on was useless baseball facts. "Well, Mr. Hollister, it appears that I continue to be in your debt." She looked toward the door, to give him the hint.

"You can start paying up right now," he said.

What? He couldn't be suggesting…that, could he? "It's time for you to leave," she said more sternly.

"Nope." He lay back on the pillow, stretched his long legs out and kicked off his boots. He folded his arms across his chest and closed his eyes.

"You can't stay here," she said, louder and with more of a shrill than she expected.

He opened one eye. "I'm tired. I've lost the better part of the evening helping you. Now, I don't care if you want to sit in that chair all night or if you decide to stretch out next to me, but I'm getting some sleep. I suggest you do the same."

"But…"

"Your virtue is safe with me. I don't date married women and I certainly don't sleep with them. And," he said, "don't get any ideas of rubbing that shampoo you've got cupped in your hands in my eyes. That would just piss me off."

She had never been so furious. Or so grateful. It was preposterous that he was bulldozing his way into her room but there was something about him that, quite frankly, made her feel safe.

She needed sleep and she didn't intend to do it in this chair. She got up, went into the bathroom to wash her hands and came back. "You don't happen to have a nail file, do you?"

He lowered his chin. "Do I look like I file my nails?" he asked, his tone low.

"Not really. I thought you were the Abominable Snowman earlier," she added. "And I guess he probably doesn't file his nails either," she finished weakly.

He laughed. It was the first time she'd heard him do that. It was nice.

He got off the bed, rummaged in the duffel bag that he'd tossed on the floor and came out with a small plastic box. He opened it and tossed a pair of clippers her direction. "Will these work?"

"Yes." She was so grateful to be able to fix her poor nails that she quickly started clipping. She put the discarded nails in a pile and, when she was finished, dumped them in the wastebasket in the corner of the room, on top of the horrible dress.

"You really messed up your hands," he said. "How did you do that?"

She was ready for the question. Had anticipated it while she was clipping. Felt good that she was functioning at a level where her brain was working again. "Bridal shower," she said. "Nasty boxes with too much tape."

"Uh-huh."

She pulled back the covers on her side and crawled in, ignoring the fact that six feet of handsome muscle was on the other side of the bed.

He reached up and turned off the light. The room was not totally dark, however, because she'd left the bathroom light on and the door halfway open.

She closed her eyes and concentrated on breathing deep. In her head, she counted. By the time she got to two hundred, he was breathing deep and she assumed he was asleep.

She thought about trying to sneak out. He'd tossed his keys on top of the chest of drawers. All she would need to do was grab them and get out without him hearing her.

She was good at that kind of thing.

Didn't know how she knew that but felt it.

But where would she go?

That was the truly terrifying part—to have no idea where her safe place was located. Where her family might be.

She didn't trust Cal Hollister but she trusted the outside world even less.

Chapter Four

Cal felt the candy bars and chips roll into him as she slid in under the covers. She smelled good. Very feminine. He had the craziest urge to reach out, to see if her skin was as soft as it looked.

But he kept his arms folded, his eyes closed, his breathing deep. She was scared. Of him. But more so of the men that he'd described. So for now, she'd filed him under the category of *lesser evil*, which was just fine with him.

When he'd seen the second Mercedes idling in the lot, hidden to the casual observer, he'd realized that she was in the middle of something big. There was some serious muscle trying to find her.

He'd considered his options. He could forget what he'd overheard and seen and be on his way. He could go to the cops. Or he could barge his way into this room and try to protect this woman.

Who was lying to him. Of that, he was confident.

But he was also pretty sure that she was scared. Really scared. And he couldn't forget those marks on her wrists.

When he'd walked in and seen her pile of clothes at the end of the bed, he'd known there was a good likelihood that she might walk out of the bathroom naked. And if he'd been a gentleman, he'd have knocked on the bathroom door, announced his presence and given her a chance to collect herself.

He'd considered that plan for about half a minute before he'd settled down on the bed, determined to let the cards fall where they may. She'd come out in her towel, which for some twisted reason was even more sexy than full nakedness. She had a compact little body. No taller than a couple inches past five feet, she had gentle curves and one set of really gorgeous legs.

When she'd walked past him, he'd seen immediately that she was holding something in her hands. But he had to admit, she was good. She'd seemed relaxed and her stride even, unhurried. Confident.

Perhaps too confident. An operative? It was possible. Since he'd heard the men's foreign accents, the thought had been nagging at him. Was she part of a foreign terrorist group intent on screwing the United States? If so, even more reason to stick close to her. Was she an innocent, caught up with the wrong people? Then she needed his help.

He listened to her breathe, knew the exact moment that she let loose and fell asleep. He waited another five minutes, then carefully propped himself up on one elbow. Examined her.

She slept daintily, with her mouth closed. Yet, she wasn't totally relaxed. Her jaw was set as if she might have her teeth together. And one hand grabbed the corner of the sheet, fingers clenched tight.

He was still worried about the lump on her head but she certainly wasn't showing any signs of concussion.

Her speech was clear, her pupils the same. Still, she should probably be checked in the night.

It was still blowing outside. That would slow the Mercedes Men down. But they would be back. He wasn't concerned for his own safety. One against four were reasonable odds for a SEAL. But his attention would be diverted by her. And that could prove fatal.

When she woke up, he was going to force her to come clean. Once he had the story, he'd know what to do.

He closed his eyes and drew in a deep breath, remembering that mango was one of his favorite fruits. A little tart. Juicy. Delicious.

Damn.

Two hours later, he gently rolled over and bumped into her, his knee to her hip. She shifted but didn't wake up. He reached up and turned on the light.

"Hey," she said. She turned to look at him. "What's going on?" she asked, her tone sleepy, yet coherent.

"Just had to use the head," he lied. He looked at her eyes. Pupils still looked good. Her color was fine. "Go back to sleep," he said, turning off the light.

She was quiet for several minutes but he could tell by her breathing that she was agitated. He wasn't surprised when she suddenly sat up in bed.

"You did not have to use the bathroom."

"I didn't?" he asked with deliberate surprise. "That's rather personal, isn't it?"

"You woke me up on purpose."

"Why would I do that? So I could have this lovely conversation?" He rolled over and gave her his back.

She waited a full minute before she shoved his shoul-

der. "You were worried about the bump on my head."
She paused. "That was nice of you," she added somewhat grudgingly.

He smiled. "Good night, Stormy."

SHE LAY IN BED, covers up to her neck, relaxed for the
first time. She knew it was because she'd finally let
down her guard. Cal had had multiple opportunities
to harm her and he'd taken none of them. Instead, he'd
disturbed his own sleep to wake her up and make sure
that she didn't have a concussion.

He was smart, cocky, a little brash. Sexy in his blue
jeans and forest-green Henley shirt.

He reminded her a little of a lounging tiger. Relaxed
yet ready to pounce. He moved with quiet confidence.

She envied that. She didn't have any confidence right
now.

But maybe by morning. She closed her eyes and let
the sleep come.

The next thing she knew, strong hands gripped her
shoulders. Half-asleep, old instincts kicked in. She
wrenched her body sideways, attempting to fight.

But she couldn't budge her attacker.

She opened her eyes, saw Cal on his knees, straddling
her.

It was several more terror-filled seconds before she
processed what was going on. She forced herself to
breathe, to clear her head. He was holding her, not hurt-
ing her, simply trying to avoid getting hurt himself. She
looked at the bedcovers. They were in a tangled heap,
wrapped around her legs.

"What day is it?" she demanded.

That surprised him. "It's Wednesday. Why?"

She let out a breath. "I needed to know if it was Saturday."

"Because?"

She didn't answer. Couldn't. But she saw the determined look on his face, knew that he wanted answers. "I had a bad dream," she said.

"You think?" he asked, his tone tense. His big body hovered over her, his weight off her but his presence immense.

While bedcovers and layers of clothes separated them, their closeness was suddenly intensely intimate. And disconcerting as hell to go from something horrible, like her dream, to something that offered a promise of being good, very good.

Breathe, she told herself.

"I think you scared ten years off my life," he said, his tone a little easier now.

"Sorry," she murmured.

He moved fast, swinging one leg over so that he was kneeling beside her. His hazel eyes looked troubled. "Want to talk about it?"

Could she? Could she go back to that dark place? Could she pretend that it had just been an oddly disturbing dream?

Could she trust this man who had barged into her room and taken up more than his share of the bed?

He'd saved her life.

Had doubled back to let her know about the men looking for her. She looked at him closer. He had a red mark on his face. He hadn't had it the night before. "What happened there?" she asked, already suspecting the truth.

"You've got a strong right hook," he said nonchalantly. "Unfortunately, you popped me one at about the same time you started screaming. It was a bit disconcerting for a minute."

Someone with less control might have killed her by mistake in response.

"I was lying on a bed," she said. "It was narrow, more like a cot."

He nodded.

"I wanted to get up, knew I needed to get away. But my wrists were tied to the bed frame. I pulled and pulled but it was no use."

"Who tied you there?" he asked.

She shook her head. "I don't know. It…it looked like a ghost. All white."

He didn't say anything.

"I know, crazy, right?" she said.

"Nope. Did the ghost talk to you?"

She thought for a minute. He had. She knew that. Couldn't remember what he'd said. "I'm not sure."

"What else do you remember?"

She pointed to the garbage can in the corner. "That was hanging in the corner of the room."

"The wedding dress?" he asked.

"Yes." She'd been scared of the dress but she could hardly admit that. There was something else and she tried desperately to recall it but it was out of her reach.

"Do you remember anything else?"

"I was sick. The ghost made me so sick."

He seemed to consider that. "You were screaming when you woke up. Why?"

"The ghost had come in and something bad was going to happen."

"What?"

"I don't know. But it was bad. I started screaming. And then…I guess I woke up."

He seemed to consider his words. "You have marks on your wrists," he said. "Like you've been restrained."

He was pointing out the obvious. She could ignore it, dismiss it. Or she could take the risk, leave herself absolutely exposed. If she didn't, she'd be all alone. "So you're saying that maybe it wasn't just a dream?"

"You tell me," he said, his voice intense.

She took a deep breath. "I'm not sure where to start."

"Maybe at the beginning."

Wouldn't that be nice? "Well, that was sometime before I met you. How long before, I'm not quite sure."

"That's a little confusing," he said.

She sat up in bed and pushed a hand through her tangled hair. "I'm in trouble. I don't know why but I am. The problem is, I don't think I can get myself out of it."

"Because?"

"Because I don't know what went wrong. I don't know who else is involved. I don't know how big this is but something tells me it's big. Really big. And that terrifies me. I don't know who the bad guys are. I don't know what they want." She took a breath.

"Okay. Anything else you don't know?"

She nodded. This was the hardest part. "When I looked in the mirror yesterday, I didn't recognize myself. Not because my hair was different or anything dumb like that. I didn't know who the woman in the mirror was." She swallowed hard. "I don't even know who I am."

Chapter Five

"I knew Mary Smith was bogus," he said.

Her dark eyes got big. "That's it? That's it?" she repeated, her voice rising. "I tell you that I don't know who I am and all you can say is 'I knew Mary Smith was bogus.' Of course it was bogus. I. Don't. Know. My. Name."

"And you're pretty freaked out about it," he said.

Now she gave him a look that would have made most people run for the door. It made him want to smile but he resisted. If he didn't watch out, she'd land another punch.

"A little," she said sarcastically.

"I get that," he said. "But I don't think it's helpful for both of us to be freaked out. And I've been around a few people who have had short-term memory loss. It comes back."

She didn't say anything for a long minute. "But what if it doesn't?"

And that simple question, asked in a small voice, pulled at his gut more than any full-blown tantrum could.

"You can't worry about that. Right now, you need to focus on staying safe." He meant that. While he was trying really hard to be calm, listening to her talk about some ghost that scared her and tied her to a bed had made him sick.

"You woke up asking the day of the week. Saturday seemed important. Why?"

"I don't know," she said, frustration in her tone. "In my dream, I knew that something very bad was going to happen on Saturday. That I had to stop it."

"Something bad to you?"

"I don't know." She shook her head. "This is going to sound crazy but even now that I'm awake, just saying the word *Saturday* makes my heart rate kick up in my chest."

"Okay. It's just Wednesday. If something bad is going to happen on Saturday, we've got a couple days. I think our best bet now is to get the hell out of Dodge," he said.

"We? Our?" she repeated. "This isn't your problem."

No, it wasn't. But he'd made his decision on that the minute he'd circled back to warn her about the Mercedes Men. "I'm between jobs right now so I've got some time on my hands."

She stared at him. He could read the questions in her eyes. She wanted to trust him but with no memory to guide her, she probably felt that any value judgment she might make was suspect. "What was your job?" she said finally.

"Navy SEAL for eight years. Got my discharge papers six months ago."

"So you haven't worked since then?"

He shook his head. "Nope. I signed on for more of the same with a private contractor. The money was really good but—" he paused "—I'm just ready for something else." There was no need to tell her that he'd come home to have a conversation with his brother, a conversation that was probably going to be difficult for both of them.

"What brought you to Missouri?" she asked.

"Family. I was raised about a hundred miles from here in a small town. Ravesville. Ever heard of it?"

"No." Her cheeks got pink. "At least I don't think I have."

He shrugged. "No worries. Don't try to force it."

She shook her head. "There are men looking for me. And I don't have any idea why. That's pretty frightening."

"I can keep you safe," he said confidently. "Now let's roll. There's a piece of apple pie in my car that we can split for breakfast."

She reached out and touched his arm. Her hand was warm and soft. "Thank you," she said softly.

She was lovely. But he couldn't forget the wedding dress that she'd wadded up in the corner wastebasket. She was someone's fiancée for sure. Maybe someone's wife. "You can have the bathroom first," he said. He had a call to make.

She got out of bed, looking like a waif in his T-shirt and sweatpants. They needed to get her some clothes, some boots. When the bathroom door closed, separating them, he reached for his phone.

Chase answered on the second ring. "Hello," he said, his tone almost a whisper.

"It's me. Cal."

There was a pause. "Are you okay?"

"Good. I'm good. You?"

"Fine." Chase took a breath. "Where the hell are you?"

"In Missouri," Cal said. "I could be at the house for dinner."

"That…that would be nice. But I'm in St. Louis. With Raney."

"Who's Raney?"

Chase laughed softly. "Don't worry. You'll get to know her. I'm going to marry her."

Cal felt a rush of emotions. He swallowed hard and managed to say in a fairly normal tone, "It's a good thing my heart is strong. Congratulations," he added.

"Thanks," Chase said. "It's a long story but Raney is testifying this week and maybe next. That's why I'm whispering. I'm at the courthouse for an early morning meeting with attorneys before testimony begins later today."

The pieces were clicking together. Raney was the witness that his brother had been protecting.

"Just as soon as she finishes, we'll be back at the house. In the meantime, you're welcome to stay. There's an extra key in the garage, in a coffee can under some nails and screws, on a shelf on the rear wall."

He laughed. "Old habits," he said. As kids, there had always been an extra key to the house somewhere in the garage. It was comforting to know that some things never changed. He thought about telling his brother about Stormy. Knew it wouldn't change Chase's mind about offering up a place to stay. But it might divert his attention from where it needed to be—on the woman who'd evidently turned the confirmed bachelor around. "I'll take you up on the offer and I'll have the coffee on when you and Raney get back."

"You do that," Chase said. He cleared his throat. "I'm really glad you're home, Cal. I'm really glad you called."

THE APPLE PIE was really good. And she enjoyed the bag of chips that came afterward. "Breakfast of champions," she said. They were in his SUV. He'd brushed the snow off and scraped the ice away and was now sitting next to her. The vehicle was warming up nicely.

The only activity at the hotel since they'd left their room was the arrival of a pickup truck that had a plow attached to the front end. The driver was clearing the parking lot again, working around the cars as best he could. He had waved as he'd taken his first pass by them but otherwise ignored them.

Cal had watched him closely for several minutes and evidently decided he wasn't any threat because he'd started in on his own breakfast. "Yep, beats an MRE any day," he said, biting into his half of the pie. "And a restaurant is out of the question right now. I don't want to take a chance on the wrong people seeing you."

The wrong people. Who the hell were they? Would she suddenly recognize them if she saw them? Maybe that would work. Maybe she should chase after the Mercedes Men and force a confrontation. It dawned on her that maybe that was exactly what Cal had planned. "Where are we going?" she asked.

"To Ravesville," he said.

"Where you grew up?" she said, remembering their earlier conversation.

"Yes. Just talked to my brother." He turned to her. "Who's engaged. Unbelievable."

She laughed. "Is he twelve?"

He frowned. "Of course not."

"Then why is it so unbelievable? People get engaged and married all the time."

He looked over his shoulder at the wedding dress

he'd retrieved from the trash can and once again thrown into the backseat. "Obviously."

Now it was her turn to stammer. "I mean…people do…but even so…I don't think I did."

He stared at her, his gaze piercing. "Why is that?" he asked finally.

"I think I would know. I think I wouldn't forget something like that."

"At the risk of stating the obvious, you don't even remember your name."

He hadn't said it unkindly. Just matter-of-fact. She totally understood his skepticism. But married? She would not have forgotten that. But it was a waste of time to dwell on it when her mind was blank. "So we're going to your family's home?"

"Yes. My brother's been living there, getting the house ready to sell. He's away right now but we can use the house."

She would be alone with this man in a strange place. She could feel her skin warm suddenly and she felt ill, as if the pie might make a return appearance. What the hell was her body trying to tell her?

Was she making a mistake? Was this the wrong thing to do?

"You look a little green," he said.

Probably because her body was trying to tell her no and her brain, which knew she had no other option, was saying *full steam ahead.*

"I'm fine," she said, dismissing his concern.

He didn't look convinced. "I imagine you'd feel better in clothes that fit. Once we get to Ravesville and you're settled at the house, I can take care of that."

The idea of him buying her clothes made her heat up

again. That was an intimate thing for a man to do for a woman. She didn't know what to say.

He didn't seem to expect an answer. Maybe he bought clothes for women all the time.

She didn't think so. He'd been a SEAL. Not a lot of department stores where they worked.

Would he ask her about sizes or simply do a visual inspection? Oh boy. She was edging toward hot.

"It normally wouldn't be that far in good weather," he said, oblivious to her temperature-control troubles. "It will take us longer today. But first there's something we need to do."

"What's that?"

"Remember last night I told you that I thought the Mercedes Men were going to come back. We need to see if I was right."

That was a bucket of ice water. "How do you propose we do that?"

"We need to get somewhere where we can see them and they can't see us."

She looked around. The palette was white with a little gray from the bare trees. But then she saw what might be a possibility. The hotel was on a service road, off the Interstate. It went for about a half mile before it reconnected with the highway.

Down the service road, about halfway to the Interstate, were two other buildings. She hadn't noticed them the previous night. Of course, it had been dark when they'd arrived. It wasn't another hotel. No, these were one-story cement structures, each with three big garage doors. The building closest to them had a partial second story made of wood, painted white, as if it had been added at some time.

From that vantage they would certainly have a good view of the hotel parking lot but would need binoculars if they wanted to see anything in detail. She realized she was tracking when he reached into the backseat, unzipped his bag and pulled out a pair. She looked at them closer. Military issue. Very nice.

"We still need to get into the building," she said.

He put the binoculars to his eyes and took a long look. When he pulled them away, he said, "There are only two cars in the parking lot for two big buildings. Both are snow-covered. I suspect the cars were there all night. Now, it's possible that somebody spent the night at work. More likely, I'd think, that the drivers were too nervous to drive their own vehicles and got a ride with a coworker."

"What if you're wrong? What if there are people inside."

He shrugged. "Hopefully, we can avoid any interaction."

"Hopefully," she said drily. "But there may be more people coming. It's a workday."

"In Missouri, two inches of snow can bring the economy to a standstill. Eight to ten inches like this is a hundred-pound gorilla. People won't be able to get out of their driveways. Anyone who can won't want to travel any farther than the local store to get bread and milk. I'm going with the relatively safe assumption that anybody who works there has the day off."

"There's still the issue of the building being locked."

He smiled. "Locked doors aren't generally too much of a problem for me. Alarm systems, now, they can be a bit trickier. Let's just hope there isn't one."

"So we're just going to drive down there, park and hope for the best?"

"Something like that," he said.

She had to admire his confidence that bordered on cockiness. And it certainly felt good to be doing something versus hiding out in a hotel room. She glanced at the road again. "A plow must have come through sometime during the night."

"At 4:18 this morning," he said, proving that she really had slept like a log once she'd finally relaxed. "The road is drifting shut again but we'll be able to get through."

It appeared the plow had done two swipes on the service road, one in and one out. It would have been a stretch to say they'd cleared both lanes. On each side of the road, snow was piled up high, probably four or five feet, making it look as if the road was a tunnel.

He was probably right. Most drivers would decide to stay home today.

She watched the plow driver finish clearing the hotel lot. "But their parking lot hasn't been plowed. We'll get stuck for sure if we try to pull in."

"I know. That's where I'm hoping we get a little luck."

"In the form of…?" She let her voice trail off.

"In the form of this guy," he said, indicating the man driving the plow. "I'm hoping that he's a smart entrepreneur and has a contract to plow out all the businesses along this service road."

That would make sense. It would make his drive to this area worthwhile. On a day like this, to a person who did that kind of work, time was money.

It took the plow driver another ten minutes to finish

Agent Bride

the hotel lot. She realized she was holding her breath as she watched him drive to the exit of the hotel. When he turned right, she let out a breath. Two minutes later, when he made another right into the other parking lot, she smiled. "Today's our lucky day," she said.

"That would be nice," Cal said. He turned off the engine. "We're going to be here a little while," he explained. "I don't want to raise suspicion if somebody looks out of their hotel room and sees us idling here for a long period."

It made sense but without heat pouring through the vents, the SUV quickly chilled and she was grateful for Cal's warm coat. Even though she'd protested, Cal had given it to her before they'd left the hotel. "No way to avoid your feet getting wet," he'd said. "I'd carry you but somebody might see it and think it looked odd. We don't want to draw any unnecessary attention."

Her feet had gotten wet on the way to the car and now they were cold. But she didn't complain.

It took another fifteen minutes before they saw the plow driver exit the parking lot, turn right and head away from them. They waited until they saw his truck merge back onto the Interstate. Then Cal started the SUV again. He put the vehicle in Drive and took off.

When they got close, she could see that the plow driver had done a pretty good job pushing the snow to the sides, although the people who owned the cars weren't going to be happy. He hadn't been as careful to go around the cars as he'd been in the hotel lot. Instead, there were big piles behind each car, effectively pinning them in.

Close-up, she realized that the two buildings were attached, similarly to how some houses were connected to garages. There was a small wooden breezeway between the two cement buildings. "That looks new," she said.

"Probably has more to do with summer than winter. Missouri gets hot and the people who work here probably want to be able to move from building to building without ever having to go outside when it's ninety-five degrees."

Just that quick, she could see herself in a sleeveless linen dress, briefcase strap over one shoulder, walking down stone steps, relishing the hot, humid air. *Don't get me wrong*, she was saying. *I'm grateful for the air-conditioning but do they have to keep it at sixty?*

Who was she talking to? Where was she?

"Stormy?" Cal asked.

She shook her head. "It's nothing," she said. She wasn't really lying. It was worth nothing.

Cal shrugged and pulled close to the building that had the second story. In addition to the three big garage doors, there was a regular door at the end closest to them. "That's our best bet," he said. "Wait here while I check it."

He got out of the SUV, moving fast. He tried the door but it didn't open. He reached into his pocket, pulled something out and went to work on the lock. Within seconds he had the door open. She was impressed. She'd jimmied open a few locked doors in her time but not that quickly.

She put her hand to her mouth. How did she know that?

The knowledge had literally just popped into her head when she'd seen the door swing open. She wanted to launch herself out of the vehicle and tell Cal that she'd remembered something that might be important.

At least it seemed more important than some vague recollection of walking down steps, conversing about the weather. However, she immediately dismissed the idea. She wouldn't offer up the information until she knew for sure what it meant.

Maybe she was a thief?

The idea sat heavy on her heart. She didn't want to wake up from this nightmare and find out that she was a bad person.

Cal stuck his head inside the building. In just seconds, he pulled back, turned, locked eyes with her and motioned for her to wait. Then he went inside, closing the door behind him.

It dawned on her that this was her chance. The keys were in the ignition, the SUV was running.

It would be easy to be on the road before he knew what was happening.

She put her hand on her door. Opened it. Drew in a breath. A mad dash around the rear of the vehicle would do it. She could slip into his seat, put the car in Drive and be on her way.

She pushed the door open enough to get one foot out. His socks were dull against the much whiter snow.

Mother Nature. Purity. In the rawest sense.

Yet it would have killed her.

If this man had not saved her.

Not once but probably twice when he'd come back to the hotel to warn her.

But if she didn't go now, it might be too late.

Chapter Six

She pulled her foot back in, closed her door and let out the breath she'd been holding. She wasn't going to steal his vehicle and leave him stranded. He didn't even have his coat.

A bad person would do that. And if she'd been bad in the past, she was turning over a new leaf, beginning immediately.

She waited another five minutes before she saw anything. Then all three of the three big garage doors that lined the front of the first building started to open. Her heart beat fast in her chest and didn't slow down until she saw Cal poke his head out of the closest opening.

He walked back to the SUV and swung into the seat. "Place is clear. I'm going to pull my SUV inside. The Mercedes Men are likely to see this building as well and may want to come take a look. I don't want to make it easy for them by leaving my vehicle in the parking lot. They've already seen it once. Unless they're really a bunch of goons, somebody is going to remember that."

He put the SUV in Reverse, not Drive. It took her just a minute to realize that he planned to back into the empty space. That was smart. Easier to get away quickly if all one had to do was pull out.

She could see that there was enough room for his SUV but that was about it. There were similar empty spaces in front of the other two garage doors. Once they got the vehicle inside and she stepped out of it, she saw that the rest of the building, which was probably the size of a football field, was filled with big boxes. "What's in all these?"

"High-end sleds. Wood toboggans. They produce in the other building and warehouse in this space. I opened one of the boxes. Quality stuff."

She started to laugh. Couldn't help it.

"What's so funny?" He pushed a button on the wall and all three garage doors closed. The space was suddenly darker, colder.

"It's like we found the Missouri branch of Santa's workshop. I'm waiting for the elves to jump out, to tell us to skedaddle, that time is a wasting and the big guy in the red suit can be a real taskmaster."

"Abominable Snowman? Elves? Santa? I'm seeing a theme here."

She nodded. Would she have her memory back by Christmas? Would she be alive at Christmas? If the Mercedes Men meant to do her harm, could she evade them for that length of time?

"Are you still going to be in Missouri at Christmas?" she asked.

"I have no idea," he said. "I'm not thinking that far out."

That was undoubtedly a good approach. She would try not to worry about anything beyond her immediate control. "What's upstairs?" she asked.

"Offices."

"Is there a good view of the hotel parking lot?"

"Yes. We won't miss them."

The stairs to the second floor were at the far right side of the building. When they got there, she realized he was right. Even without the binoculars, they could probably see what was going on. With the binoculars, they could pick out fine detail.

Good. She wanted a close-up look at the men. If life was fair, she'd have an epiphany of sorts and know exactly who she was. A couple things had already popped into her head. Perhaps…she looked around…perhaps a visual would be the push that got the sled going down the hill at warp speed.

"Don't touch anything," he said. "We don't want to leave any fingerprints behind, just in case."

She sat in one of the chairs, with her hands folded together, resting on her lap. The office was warm and soon she was nodding off. She got up, took off Cal's big coat and started walking around the room to stay awake. "I need something to do. I'm going crazy."

He was slouched in the chair, arms behind his head, feet crossed at the ankles. "How about sports trivia? What year did Tiger Woods begin golfing professionally?"

"That's easy—1996."

"Your turn," he said.

She studied him. "The first World Cup was held in what country in 1930?"

"Uruguay," he said. "How many wins did Muhammad Ali have?"

"Fifty-six wins. Five defeats," she added.

"There's no extra credit," he teased. "Who did Wayne Gretzky play for in the 1980s?"

"Edmonton Oilers. Who is the only pitcher to lead

both the National and the American League in shut-outs, in the same season?"

He scratched his chin. "CC Sabathia. Played for the Indians, then the Brewers." He smiled at her.

"You're really good," she said.

"You're not so bad yourself," he said. He was quiet for a few minutes. "There are a lot of women broadcasting professional sports these days. Do you think that might be your job? Or maybe you're a sportswriter."

"Just the idea of standing up in front of a camera and talking to thousands of people makes my knees shake. I don't think that's my job. I suppose I could be a writer. I feel like that's more realistic but it still doesn't seem right."

"Okay. Maybe you're just a sports geek. We're trying to make lemonade out of grapefruit."

She sat back down. "We could have slept longer," she said.

"Yep. But I didn't like the idea of being surprised by your cousins."

"I don't think we're family."

"I hope not," he said. "It's going to be a real buzz killer if you see them and the first thought that comes to your head is what you're supposed to bring to Thanksgiving dinner."

She stared out the window. "Thanksgiving. Is that why you're headed home?"

"Yep. A few months ago, I decided that this was going to be the year…the year I joined my brothers for Thanksgiving dinner."

"You told me about your brother Chase. How many others?"

"Just one. Brayden. Everybody calls him Bray. He's

four years older than Chase, seven years older than me. He left for the marines when I was in middle school. Now he's a DEA agent and lives in New York." He was silent for a minute. "It will be good to see them," he added.

It wasn't all that unusual for family to get together on holidays but the way he said it, she had the distinct feeling that there was more to the story. She wanted to ask but decided not to. She settled for something less personal. "Do you cook?"

"Uh, no. Not really. You?"

She tried to remember if she liked to cook. Had no idea. "I will definitely be out of your hair by Thanksgiving," she said instead.

He shrugged. "Thanks for not driving off earlier."

She stared at him. "You left the keys on purpose. It was a test, wasn't it?" she challenged.

"I figured it was better for both of us if we knew the answer to the question early on."

"The question being, will she run if she gets the chance?"

"Exactly. At least here, I had access to heat and there's more snacks in the vending machines. There are lots worse places to be stranded."

She wanted to be angry, to be outraged that he'd baited her. But something told her that she would have done the very same thing. She stood silently, watching out the window. Finally, she turned to him. "Where exactly were those vending machines?"

He laughed but quickly silenced it when they saw two Mercedes sedans drive into the hotel parking lot. He put the binoculars up to his eyes.

With her naked eye, she could see that no one got

out of the one car. They parked in the back row, facing out, so that they had a good view of the office. Two men got out of the other car that had taken a front-row parking space.

"Do you think the clerk is in danger?" she whispered, before realizing how foolish that was. The men couldn't hear them. Now that it was happening, now that the men were actually back, it made her chest feel tight. What the hell did they want with her? If they had bad intent, was it possible that innocent bystanders would be caught in the fray? That was unacceptable.

"I thought of that," he said. "I don't think so. A dead hotel desk clerk in the middle of Missouri will get some attention. Every hotel in the state will be on hyperalert. It would seriously hamper their abilities to inquire about you at other places. I think they'll use other means of persuasion to get his attention."

"A new cell phone?" she asked drily. "Unlimited downloads?"

He smiled and handed her the binoculars. "My guess is old-fashioned cash. Take a good look at the two men when they come out of the office."

"You're awfully confident that the clerk will show them the rooms?"

"He's barely voting age and certainly no match for these guys. He'll take the cash and when they tell him to keep his mouth shut about it, he probably will because not only would he lose his job, he'll have to worry about these guys finding him and that their weapon of choice will no longer be Ben Franklins."

"Is that what you'd do?" she asked.

He shook his head. "Hell, no. I'd lead them both into an empty room and take them out. Then I'd wait for the two goons in the car to get impatient and come check on why their friends are no longer visible. Then I'd take those two down."

If another man had made that boast, she'd consider it false bravado. But Cal said it factually, without emotion, as if it was all in a day's work.

Navy SEALs were well trained. That was a given. And, she suspected, very confident of their abilities. Otherwise, they wouldn't have the guts to do what routinely needed to be done.

The door of the hotel office opened. She stared through the binoculars. The Mercedes Men walked on each side of the front desk clerk, who hadn't even thought to put on a coat. He would be freezing by the time they looked at every room.

Cold but hopefully alive. She stared at the faces of the men, waiting for some memory to return. But there was nothing. She could see the scar that Cal had described. It was very noticeable and seemed familiar. Why, however, was beyond her grasp. She studied the shorter man. The way he walked, how he swung his leg from the hip, was eerily familiar.

"Know them?" Cal asked.

"Both the scar and the way the other one is walking seem familiar. But I'm wondering if it's because you mentioned both things last night when you described them. Maybe I pictured that and now I think I've seen it before." She looked at him. "I think I've lost my confidence to sort out what is real and what isn't."

"Okay," he said.

"You say it like it's no big deal," she said, angry at herself. "I don't know any more than I knew ten minutes ago. We wasted all this time."

"It was a long shot," he said, "that simply seeing them would jump-start your memory. One we probably needed to take but not the basket to put all our eggs into. I got what I needed."

"And what was that?"

"I wanted to verify that the two cars were still traveling together and that they hadn't split up. I think we can assume that this is going to be their pattern. One car and two men are always backup. I also wanted to see how long it took them to come back. It was about six o'clock when they were here last night. It's almost noon. That's eighteen hours. I think we have to assume that they probably took turns sleeping so that they didn't lose any time looking. It gives me a feel for how they've identified their search area."

"They're looking for a needle in a haystack. Even if I had been out there somewhere, in the dark, in the snow, it would have been virtually impossible to find me."

"I know. But they kept looking. That gives me some idea of how determined they are."

"This is absolutely crazy," she said, watching the desk clerk knock on doors. If no one came to the door, the clerk would unlock the door, the men would step inside, only to reemerge a minute later. Some of the rooms were occupied. When the knock was answered, there was a brief conversation before the two men stepped inside, out of view. Like before, in less than a minute, they'd be back. "What do you think they're saying to the guests?"

"I suspect it's some line about the men being inspectors of some sort and they have to make a quick visual inspection of the room. The guests are probably irritated but as long as the men get in and out quickly, will probably not make too big a fuss."

"Good. If they do, this could turn ugly." And that would be on her conscience forever.

The men looked at all eight rooms on the first floor and started upstairs. "Are we going to stay until they finish?" she asked.

"We have to. We can't risk the men in the second car seeing us leave."

But that would make them sitting ducks if the men decided to search the warehouse next.

She watched as the trio made progress. The hotel clerk had his arms wrapped around himself and he looked miserably cold. The other two men, in their big black coats and dark pants, simply looked miserable. They both had square faces and flat noses.

"Do you think they might be brothers?" she asked, handing him back the binoculars.

He watched for a few minutes. "I think you're probably right," he said. "I didn't see that right away because I was focused on the one guy's stride."

They watched in silence for a few minutes. The trio got to the door of the room where she and Cal had spent the night. They knocked. Waited. Opened the door.

If Cal had not come back to warn her, she might still be in the room, oblivious to the fact that danger was on her heels. "Thank you," she said. "I probably can't say it enough."

"You'd have done the same for me," he said.

She liked to think so. The men came out. Checked the final two rooms. Their mouths were set and their posture tense. The trio walked back toward the office.

Please, just go, she thought. She did not want the young hotel clerk harmed.

She let out her breath when the men returned to their car and the young man went back inside the office. They were leaving. She was grateful.

Until she realized that the Mercedes Men were headed toward the warehouse. She and Cal had nowhere to go.

Chapter Seven

Cal moved quickly. "I'm going downstairs. Stay up here. No matter what, stay up here."

"What are you going to do?"

"Whatever it takes," he said. He grabbed the coat that Stormy had shed and tossed it at her. "Lock this door behind me. Hide in that closet," he said, pointing across the room.

"Shouldn't we call 911?"

"Won't do us any good. By the time they get here, it's going to be over, one way or the other." He could tell she didn't like the sound of that.

"But—"

"No time," he said. The Mercedes Men were half-way down the road. He pulled up his pant leg, reached inside his cowboy boot and came out with the knife that he kept strapped to his ankle. He pressed a button on the handle and the blade extended. He handed it to her.

She didn't recoil or throw up her hands. She took it, tested the weight in the palm of her hand, then gripped the handle.

"Do you think you could stab someone?" he asked.

"I'll do what I have to do."

"Good. If anybody besides me opens that closet door,

let them get close and then go for center body mass. Don't hesitate. You'll only get one chance."

He took two steps toward the door.

"Cal," she said.

He turned and she was close. Close enough to reach her arms up, pull his face toward her and kiss him hard. It was unexpected and explosively hot. He opened his mouth and their tongues battled.

When she pulled back, he felt as if he'd been hit by an incoming missile. Dazed.

"Be careful," she said.

He was generally never careful but almost always successful. "I'll do my best," he managed.

He ran lightly down the stairs. If the Mercedes Men followed their pattern, two would enter. He would have the advantage of surprise. It would be enough unless one of them got off a lucky shot. The trick was letting them get far enough inside that the other men waiting in the car didn't realize that their buddies were under attack and come running. That would change the odds.

He absolutely could not let any of them get upstairs. While the knife gave Stormy a bit of protection, it was an inefficient weapon against a gun.

He stood flat against the wall, near the door that they would either pick the lock or simply knock down. He listened hard. Could hear the first set of tires. The car engine. Second set of tires. That engine. Then nothing for a minute.

Car door slam. Second car door slam.

He breathed normally, in and out, in and out. He needed to get steady fast. Needed to get that kiss out of his head.

His buddies would be laughing their tails off knowing that his knees were practically knocking together. Not because of the Mercedes Men. Them he could handle.

The doorknob jiggled. It had been an easy door to unlock. If they had any skill at it, it shouldn't take them long.

He listened for the lock to tumble.

What he heard was a muffled cry, the voice deep. Then fast conversation at the door in a language that he didn't know. Then the sound of running feet. Two car doors. Engines changing gears.

The cars were both leaving.

What the hell?

Then it made sense. He heard the sound of another approaching vehicle, coming from the direction of the hotel. Big rumbling engine.

The engines from the two cars were fading. They'd turned right out of the parking lot, headed back toward the Interstate.

He needed to see. He ran back upstairs to the windows.

It was a big delivery truck. The sign on the side said Wardman Toboggan Company.

It was a "good news, bad news" kind of moment.

Good news in that the Mercedes Men had decided a confrontation wasn't in their best interests. Bad news in that the likelihood that the truck would pull into the garage and see their rental car was pretty high.

He'd had no compunction about taking out the Mercedes Men but didn't want to have that same fight with an unsuspecting employee.

"Change of plans," he said, turning. Then smiled when Stormy didn't immediately open the closet door. Good girl. "Just me," he said. "Mercedes Men backed off when a company truck started down the road. Let's roll. We need to be in our vehicle and ready to go if those garage doors open."

She opened the closet door and tried to hand him back the knife. "You keep it," he said.

She shrugged, retracted the blade and put it into the pocket of his coat that she'd once again put on. She didn't ask any additional questions, just followed him down the stairs and got inside the SUV. He could hear the engine of the truck. It needed a tune-up.

He started the SUV. Counted to five. The garage doors started rising. All three of them. He saw the nose of the big truck in front of the third door. Waited until the door in front of the SUV was open far enough that they could squeeze under.

Gunned it. And they were out of the building and sliding around the edge of the big warehouse, likely before the man in the truck had any idea what had happened.

He went the opposite direction of the Mercedes Men, heading back toward the hotel. But he didn't stop there. Just kept going until he was also back on the Interstate.

She didn't say a word until they were safely back on the road with nobody following them. "That was fun," she said.

He turned, trying to figure out if she was being sarcastic. He didn't think so.

It was oddly endearing and very attractive. "Ready for the drive?" he asked.

"Sure. But what about the people at Wardman's?"

"Well, I suspect it'll go sort of like this. When they first saw my SUV pulling out, they probably would have tried to figure out if there was a legitimate reason for me to be inside. For example, did the SUV belong to someone who works there? When they came up empty on that, they might have tried to get a plate number. But they wouldn't have. We got out of there pretty fast and this morning before we started, I made sure there was a nice mud and snow mix on the plates, obscuring the information."

"They'll call the police?" she said, more fact than question.

"I imagine so. First, they'll call the boss. He or she will tell them to call the police. Then there will a quick look around to see if anything is missing or disturbed. When everything looks okay, they'll probably calm down, and quite frankly, the cops won't put any time into it."

"Cameras?" she asked.

"Didn't see any. Those are getting more sophisticated by the minute, however, so it's possible. Nervous about seeing your photo splashed across the internet or the local news station?"

"Nervous?" She put her hands on the borrowed sweatpants. "Why, do these make me look fat?"

He laughed so hard that he almost couldn't drive. He might not know her name but he was slowly fitting together the pieces of Stormy. And liking the image he was creating.

Which was a problem considering she was somebody else's woman.

He turned on the radio. "I'm going to try to catch some road reports," he said.

SHE WATCHED THE miles roll by. They'd left the Interstate behind and turned off onto a two-lane highway.

In most places, it was plowed wide enough to cause no worry for cars going opposite directions. There were places where it had blown badly and had they met a car in exactly those spots, it might have been an interesting game of chicken.

That didn't happen. In fact, they met very few cars. Fewer than ten so far and none of them had been a black Mercedes.

The lack of activity gave her plenty of time for reflection. Perhaps too much.

She'd kissed him. Couldn't put it out of her mind.

She'd grabbed his face, pulled him close and laid one on him. What the heck did that tell her about the kind of person she was?

She was a kisser? A wanton kisser? A nondiscriminating kisser, looking for any pair of available lips?

Or was it possible that she was very discriminating and had simply found something unique and interesting and worth her time? That was certainly something to chew on.

She fought the urge to ask Cal how he felt about it. That would have been such a female thing to do—to want to talk it to death. He hadn't resisted. Had participated quite nicely, in fact.

But hadn't mentioned it and apparently wasn't inclined to want to talk about it or anything else. He'd fiddled with the radio for a few minutes and settled on a talk radio station that was debating the use of drone technology in the public sector.

She could tell the roads were still slick although no new snow was falling. Once the plows and the salt trucks were out and about, it would be fine to travel. There would be nothing to slow down the Mercedes Men.

But how would they be able to trace her to Ravesville? Maybe once she got to Cal's family home, she'd truly be safe. Her mind would heal.

She'd had the two flashes of memory. They seemed incongruent. Her in a pretty dress with a briefcase and the ability to pick a lock. Figuring out how these seemingly disjointed memories went together was difficult.

Equally challenging was sorting through the new information that she was learning. Just this morning, she'd discovered two rather interesting facts. One, when Cal had handed her the knife and told her not to hesitate, she'd known that she would do what she had to do to protect herself. She would fight. And the second thing that had become abundantly clear when she'd been hiding in the closest, sweltering in Cal's big coat, was that she didn't like being left behind. When Cal had ordered her to hide, her first impulse had been to tell him to think again. But she'd decided to go along.

While she'd been waiting, her heart had been beating hard. At first, she'd thought it was in fear. Then she'd realized that it was in anticipation.

Of what, she wasn't sure. But she wasn't scared of it.

She wasn't scared now. She closed her eyes, comfortable in the warm SUV, confident that Cal could handle the roads just fine.

She woke up when she felt a gentle tap on her shoulder. She opened her eyes.

"We're getting close," he said. "Thought you might want to get a glimpse of the town. We have to go through it to get to the house."

"Will anyone recognize you?"

"I wouldn't think so. I haven't been home since my mom died eight years ago."

"Did you…did you see her before she passed?"

"I did. We had a couple days together. She was in and out because of the meds they had given her but it was still good." He was silent for a few more minutes. "Where do your parents live?" he asked.

"Fort Collins, Colorado," she said. Then turned to him. "How the heck do I know that?" she asked, hysteria hovering at the edge of her very slim grasp on sanity. She closed her eyes. Then after a long, frustrating moment opened them again. "This is crazy. I can't picture them and I don't know their names but I'm confident that it's Fort Collins. How can this be?"

He shrugged. "I'm not a physician but I've seen this before. When you try to force it, it won't come. But random things will be there. It should make you feel good, that it's not all gone."

She rubbed her forehead. "It's like my brain is a crossword puzzle and the edges have been rubbed off the pieces so I can't see how everything fits together."

"It'll come," he said. He slowed the vehicle down. "Well, this is it. Don't blink or you'll miss it."

She smiled. It was sort of charming. A big main street, a couple blocks long, with four-way stop signs at the end of every block. Lots of red brick. Diagonal parking. There were a few cars in front of the Wright Here, Wright Now Café. She looked in the windows as they passed. "Cute little place," she said.

"Uh-huh."

"You lived here your whole life?"

"Yep."

"Your mom and dad must have liked the community."

He didn't answer right away. Two stop signs later, he said, "My dad died when I was eleven."

"I'm sorry," she said.

"My mom remarried a couple years later. Brick Doogan. He wasn't a nice guy. He's been living in the house since Mom died. He was in a fatal car accident very recently."

"Which is why your brother is fixing up the house to sell."

"So you were listening?" he teased. "I'm not sure what the house will look like. I got the impression from Chase when we first spoke about it that it was worse than he expected."

"It's got to be better than a snowdrift," she said.

He nodded. "A woman with low expectations. My kind of girl."

She felt her stomach tighten. His kind of girl. Was she?

As nice as that might be, there was a reason she could not be involved with Cal. Felt it. Sadly enough, knew it had something to do with the wedding dress in the backseat.

Chapter Eight

As they passed the Fitzler house, he pointed it out. "Gordy Fitzler and his wife have lived there forever. They had two daughters. They were older than me but that didn't stop me from teasing them mercilessly on the school bus. Gordy owned a roofing company and Chase worked for him for several years."

"Is that a for-sale sign?" she asked.

Cal squinted. The sign was in the front yard and the snow was high enough to almost obscure it. But Stormy was right. The Fitzlers were selling. "I wonder if that will hurt our chances of making a sale, to have two houses on the same road up for sale at the same time."

"Or maybe help it. Someone will come out to see this house and it won't be quite right and then they'll realize your house is for sale, too."

"Maybe. Fitzler has a nice outbuilding that he used for his business. That may make his a more attractive property."

He drove another five hundred yards. "That's ours."

"It's big," she said.

"Big enough," he said. There'd been times in the past years when his whole living space wasn't as big as one of the rooms in this rambling white farmhouse.

The driveway to the house was drifted badly and even with his big SUV and a running start, Cal thought there was a possibility that they might get stuck. But he wasn't inclined to leave his vehicle on the road and walk the rest of the way.

So he accelerated, made the turn and tried to plow through it. The back end slid and the tires grabbed. He didn't let up on the gas and managed to get close to the house before the vehicle stopped forward progress.

He looked at Stormy and at her feet in his white athletic socks. "I'll carry you," he said. "Let me get the key out of the garage first."

He pushed open his own door, stomped through the snow and then used his hands and feet to move snow away from the side door of the garage. When he could get it open, he slipped inside. Flipped the light on and from there, it was easy to find the key. Just where Chase had said it would be.

He grabbed a shovel on his way out and noted with relief that there was a snowblower. That was new. When he and his brothers had lived here, they'd shoveled. Missouri rarely got snow like this so it hadn't been all that difficult.

Today, he sincerely hoped the sucker worked.

He waded back to the car, got Stormy's door open, and gathered her up in his arms. His coat came almost to her knees and he knew it had never smelled better, some combination of hotel lotion and Stormy.

There was a moment of excitement when he got to the steps and his foot sunk deeper than expected. He pitched forward. "Whoa?" he said.

She squealed. It was delicate and feminine and it made him laugh.

"Sorry about that," he said. He yanked his foot free and managed to get up onto the porch, where the snow was significantly less.

"Put me down so you can unlock the door," she said.

He ignored her. Instead he shifted her so that one hand was free. Unlocked the door and pushed it open with his foot. Stepped inside the dark cold house, still holding her.

She stretched out a leg and used her toes to flip up the light switch.

When light flooded the entryway, he grinned at her. "We're a good team," he said. Then he carefully set her down.

The house was much the same yet felt very different than the last time he'd been there, when it had been filled with death. It smelled different. The light seemed different.

Chase had been busy. The living room and dining room both had fresh paint. The carpet in the dining room had been ripped up, exposing a real nice wood floor that he hadn't realized was there. There was a neat pile of wood flooring in the corner of the living room, a good match to the dining room, just waiting to be laid down.

He walked toward the kitchen with Stormy following. He remembered the appliances. White, sturdy, and more than thirty years old, they'd been a part of Hollister dinners since before he was born. The table was the same, too. But the kitchen felt warmer, more welcoming than he remembered it feeling eight years ago. Maybe it was the paint? It was different. Maybe it was because it was sparkling clean?

Maybe it was because Stormy was beside him?

He shook his head to clear it. He might have carried her over the threshold but she was somebody else's bride.

"Great house," she said. "I love the big windows."

"The one in the front room was replaced about seventeen years ago. After my stepfather put my hand through it. My punishment."

He heard her gasp and immediately regretted his frankness. It was unexpected, really. He was generally much more careful about sharing anything personal. But somehow his usual defenses were on the fritz when it came to Stormy.

"What did you do?"

"Didn't get the dirty clothes off my bedroom floor quite fast enough."

She was silent for a few minutes. "How old were you?" she asked.

"Fourteen."

Another bout of silence. "I'm sorry that happened to you," she said finally.

He appreciated that she didn't seem inclined to want more information. Such as how did that make him feel about his stepfather? His mother? What was it like after that? Those were complex questions with even more complex answers.

"So that makes you thirty-one," she said. "I wondered. You must have gone to college before you enlisted?"

"Chase and I moved to St. Louis the day I turned eighteen. He got a job with the St. Louis Police Department. Busted his ass so that I could go to school and get an engineering degree."

"And then you decided to enlist? After all that? And become a SEAL?"

"Seemed like the thing to do." He wasn't going to tell her about the conversation that he'd had with Brick Doogan, about how the man had tossed his world upside down in a matter of minutes.

He hadn't had the guts to confront Chase with the truth at the time. Had simply left home and proved time and time again that he was tough enough to take anything that got thrown at him. Proved that nothing scared him.

"Now what?" she asked.

"I'm going to go see if the snowblower works. The car needs to be dug out." He thought that they were safe in Ravesville but he wasn't taking any chances on getting caught unawares with no means of escape.

"What should I do?" she asked.

"Whatever you want," he said, smiling. "You're a guest."

An uninvited guest. For sure.

He had to be regretting that he'd ever pulled her out of the snowdrift. Yet he was being really great about it. Acting as if it was no big deal that he was suddenly saddled with a woman who didn't even know her own name but apparently had done something to give four guys a reason to chase her around the Missouri countryside.

She was going to remember everything and get the heck out of his hair. She was.

She had to.

The alternative was too awful to contemplate.

But in the meantime, she could earn her keep. She was hungry. He had to be more so. So far, she'd seen him consume a good amount of licorice, chips, candy bars and apple pie.

She suspected that wasn't all he normally ate. He was incredibly buff. He'd picked her up and *carried* her several times, as if she weighed twenty pounds rather than a hundred and twenty pounds.

At thirty-one, he was young to have lost both of his parents. And his stepfather, too, although the man certainly didn't sound like a prize. What kind of person shoved a fourteen-year-old's hand through a window?

Her stomach grumbled, reminding her that it was time to eat. She walked over to the cupboards and started opening them. There was a good supply of the staples: flour, sugar, salt, dried pasta and cereal. She opened the refrigerator. It was practically bare. No eggs, no milk, none of the things that would allow her to cook much of anything.

She heard the roar of the snowblower and knew that Cal would be occupied for a little while. There was a lot of snow. She looked again at the cupboards. She was going to have to figure out how to deliver on her end, as well.

Ten minutes later, she was waiting for water to boil. Something about standing at the stove felt familiar. Was she a cook? Did she spend time in the kitchen? She closed her eyes, willing her mind to find something that would tell her just one small thing about her past.

But it was as if she'd been born yesterday, in the middle of a snowstorm, wearing a wedding dress. But she hadn't been. She had parents. And she'd remembered that they lived in Fort Collins, Colorado. If she got really desperate, maybe she could put a picture of herself in the paper with the hopes that they'd see it. Sort of like a lost-cat advertisement.

She shook her head. She was really starting to feel sorry for herself, wasn't she? Enough of that. It was going to get her nowhere.

She opened two cans of tomato sauce. She added a liberal amount of dried basil, oregano and garlic. She found a jar of mushrooms and threw those in, as well.

Then she opened the freezer, saw the frozen rolls and grabbed them. By the time Cal came back inside, she'd set the table and there was a steaming bowl of spaghetti and warm bread from the oven. She'd poured them both water to drink.

He was snow-covered and his jeans were wet. He sniffed the air. "Smells great," he said.

It felt good to do something for him, even if it was as simple as throw a quick meal together. "So the snow-blower worked?"

"After a little gentle coaxing," he said, shedding his coat.

"You must be the handy type," she said.

"My background is mechanical engineering. I'm a total geek."

"You don't look like a geek," she said, immediately wishing she'd kept her thoughts to herself.

"Oh yeah?" He lifted his chin.

In his faded blue jeans that he wore low on his hips and his flannel shirt, he looked sexy and just a little dangerous. The cold air hung around him and his cheeks and nose were red from the wind.

"I always loved figuring out how things worked. Mechanical engineering was an easy choice. After I enlisted, I realized that I had something I could offer to the rest of the guys on the team. As long as I had some string, duct tape and a sharp knife, I could get most anything running again."

"Good skill," she said.

He sniffed the air again. "Looks as if you've got your own skills."

"It's just a little something," she said. "But it's ready if you are."

He followed her into the kitchen, washed his hands and sat down at the table. He looked up at her. "This is amazing," he said, as if she'd done something special. She felt warm.

"Thanks," she said. "We're going to need to get some milk, eggs and fresh produce at some point."

"No problem," he said, taking a big serving of the spaghetti. "I'll go to town tomorrow," he said. "Just make me a list."

He said it as if he expected her to stay. "I might remember everything by tomorrow," she said.

He nodded. "I hope you do."

"I'll be out of your hair just as soon as I do," she said.

"Okay."

"And if…if it doesn't come back," she added, realizing that she needed to vocalize her greatest fear, "I'll still move on. I know this is just a temporary stop," she said, assuring him that she wasn't going to overextend her welcome.

"Great," he said.

She laid down her fork. "I know I'm putting you at risk by being here."

He sighed. "Do I look concerned about that?"

She shook her head. "Maybe you should be," she said. "Maybe you should just tell me to get the hell out."

He looked at his half-eaten lunch. "When you can cook like this? You think I'm crazy?"

Maybe. He was inviting trouble into his life. "I just want to be clear on my intentions," she said stiffly.

"Crystal clear," he said. He pointed at the bread basket. "Can you pass the rolls?"

AFTER LUNCH, THEY cleared the table. He washed and she dried the dishes. "Let's take a look at the rest of the house," he said.

There was a master bedroom off to the side of the kitchen. It had also been freshly painted but there wasn't a stick of furniture in it. The attached bath had been cleaned and emptied of all signs of Brick.

He wondered if that had been the first thing that Chase had done. It wasn't as if Chase didn't have a reason to hate Brick Doogan, to want to exorcize his spirit from the premises. He'd taken the brunt of Brick's hateful nature, protecting everyone else in the house.

Cal had let him. And that knowledge still rubbed him raw with guilt.

When he and Stormy went upstairs, it was easy to see that Chase had plans for the second story but had not yet had time to implement them. Bray's room was empty save a gallon of new paint in an unopened can. He opened Bray's closet. It was filled with old winter coats. He recognized them as coats his mother had worn over a period of many years. She'd been dead for over eight years and Brick still hadn't done anything with them.

Maybe he'd been sentimental. Maybe he'd simply been lazy. It didn't matter but perhaps one of them would fit Stormy.

Chase's room was also empty and his closet was bare. There was a gallon of paint there, as well.

He was starting to get the pattern. He wasn't surprised when he opened the door to his old room and saw the gallon of paint. The bed in the middle of the room did give him pause. There was no frame. The mattress and box springs sat on the floor. Sheets and a blanket, looking freshly washed, were folded and sitting at the end of the bare mattress. He opened the closet door. Women's clothes and men's clothes.

Not his mother's or Brick's. These belonged to Chase and Raney. He turned to Stormy. "Will any of these fit?"

She glanced at several of the items, looking at the size tags. "Well enough," she said. "But I hate to use someone's things without their permission."

He shook his head. "Chase won't care and while I don't know Raney, if my brother loves her, then she's the type who won't care, as well."

She nodded. "I suppose you would like your sweatpants back," she said.

His sweatpants and T-shirt had never looked or smelled better. "I'm glad they served a purpose," he said. "I'll let you have some privacy to pick something out." See, he could be a gentleman. Even when his libido was spiking at the mere thought of her getting naked to change clothes.

When she nodded, he walked out of the bedroom and went downstairs. The fifth stair squeaked, the way it always had. It brought back a sudden rush of memories. Being fourteen or fifteen, waiting for his brother to come home. Hoping that Chase would get inside without Brick hearing that he was late or realizing that he'd been drinking. And he'd cringe when he heard the step squeak, wishing that Chase had been more careful, wishing that Brick slept more soundly.

And then digging deeper under the covers when Chase and Brick would go at it. There'd be yelling and then worse when Brick stopped talking and got his point across with his hands.

He'd just lain there. Afraid.

And later, when he got Chase alone and begged him to be more careful, his brother had just smiled.

He'd been such a dumb ass that he'd never even questioned why Brick went after Chase with a vengeance and left him alone. Until Brick had told him why.

That was the day everything changed.

But that was more than eight years ago and he needed to forget it. If not forget it, then at least get past it. That was why he had come home for Thanksgiving.

He sat down on the couch in the living room and watched the road. There was generally little traffic on the rural road and none today. The sun was shining and made the living room, with its big windows, feel warmer than the rest of the house.

He closed his eyes and let himself relax. He was home. For better or worse. Back in Ravesville.

Five minutes later, he heard the upstairs bedroom door open and close. Then light steps on the stairs. He smiled when Stormy came into view.

She'd put on a blue jean skirt, a black sweater and black knee-high boots. She had some kind of black nylons or tights on, too. She looked fabulous. Sexy.

Maybe she should have stayed in his T-shirt and sweatpants. *Married*, he reminded himself. Or close to it.

"Looks as if the clothes fit pretty well," he said.

"They're wonderful. I had underestimated the psychological boost of having clothes on that actually fit."

Psychological boost for her maybe. Psychological torture for him. "What do you want to do with your bridal gown?" he asked, needing to quickly get his head back in the game.

She looked startled. "I…I don't know."

"I don't think we should leave it in the SUV. If we need to abandon that vehicle quickly, I don't want to have to deal with it."

She nodded. "Of course. I guess we should bring it inside." She paused. "I don't want it," she added. She pointed at the brick fireplace on the far side of the room. "I suspect it would burn pretty well."

He stared at her. "How can you be so sure that the dress isn't important to you, that it isn't a good thing?"

She shrugged. "I don't know how to explain it. All I can say is that I think I would know if I was recently married. I would feel it."

Not the best logic he'd ever heard.

"I'm not wearing a ring," she said.

He knew that. He'd checked, of course. "You don't have any rings on. Maybe you're the type that doesn't like jewelry."

She studied her hands. She'd clipped her nails very short to repair the damage. Still, her hands were very feminine, with long, graceful fingers. When she looked up, he could see the frustration in her eyes.

"There's something not right about that," she said.

"About what?"

"I have a ring. A favorite ring. Silver. Wide band. Heavy. I can see it. But I don't have any idea how I got it or where it is now." She sighed. "I swear, I want to just claw my brain apart."

He laughed. "Well, it's a good thing, then, that you can't get to it. Don't push it. It's something that you can remember the ring. The rest will come." He stood up. "I'll get your wedding dress. I don't think we should burn it. There may be evidence on it that shouldn't be destroyed."

"I guess I could hang it in the closet upstairs."

He shrugged. "Maybe we shouldn't be so quick to push it aside."

"I'm not sure I'm following."

"Do you know if it was a new dress or do you think it had been borrowed from someone?"

He could tell the question surprised her. She closed her eyes. "It was hanging on a white padded hanger, the kind you might find in a wedding dress store. There are straps inside some dresses… I don't know what they're called, but you use them if you're hanging up a dress that has a wide neckline and won't fit on a hanger very well. Somebody had hung the dress on the hanger using those straps. They were perfectly wrapped. I never saw a tag but I think it's very possible that it was new." She opened her eyes. "Where are you going with this?"

"Stores sell certain brands of clothing. Even wedding dress stores, right? By looking at the brand, do you think it's possible that we might identify the store that it came from?"

"Maybe. But I'm pretty sure that I didn't go there and pick it out. They aren't going to be able to tell me anything about me."

"But one of the Mercedes Men must have picked it

up. They would have paid for it, maybe with a credit card. Maybe we can find out something about them."

"We don't have much else to go on," she admitted. "But where would we start?"

"We know where you ended up. We have to work off the assumption that they didn't get you into a wedding dress and put you on a plane. We can use my phone to search for all the bridal stores in Missouri. Then we call them to see if they carry this particular brand."

"That could work," she said. "But there could be several. It's a big state, maybe a popular brand."

"We'll start with those that are closest to us. Ready to try?"

She nodded. "If I thought standing on my head in the corner would help, I'd try that."

Chapter Nine

According to the pink tag sewn into the back of the dress, it was a Jenna McCoy. That meant nothing to her.

But when they searched the brand, they realized that it was carried by seventeen bridal stores in the state of Missouri. And upon further investigation, they realized that there were more bridal stores in the state that didn't list their labels.

It was daunting to say the least. "Seventeen that we know about," she said.

"Eight if we consider the major markets of Kansas City, Colombia and St. Louis. Those are the closest geographically to where you were found."

"Eight," she repeated. "Do we call them and describe the dress? See if they've recently sold one?"

"That might work. Maybe we could get a contact name and email address and send them a photo?"

"I think they're going to think we're nuts. I can just hear them now. *Hey, lady, you got the dress. Why the heck don't you know where you bought it?*"

"I never said it was a perfect plan."

She couldn't help it. She laughed. He was going for innocent and it was a look that he simply couldn't pull off. "Let me think about this," she said. "In the meantime, I'm going to make dessert."

"A real dessert?"

He might not be able to do innocent but he could do hopeful really well.

"You'll see," she said and left him alone in the living room.

In the kitchen, she found a can of cherry pie filling and a can of crushed pineapple. She opened them, mixed them together in a 9x13 pan and spread a box of cake mix on top. She dotted it with butter she found in the refrigerator. She was just opening the oven when Cal called out, "How's it going in there?"

"Good. Forty-five minutes," she said.

"It's been about five years since I've had homemade dessert. I guess I can wait a little longer."

He said it lightheartedly but it reminded her of the tremendous sacrifice that soldiers made. She wiped her hands on a towel and walked back into the living room. He was sitting on the couch, looking at his cell phone.

"Thank you for your service," she said, her tone serious. "I imagine it was difficult at times."

He nodded. "Sure. Difficult. Wonderful. Frustrating. Exhilarating. Any given day it was different. Sometimes any given hour. Got to see a fair amount of the world."

She laughed. "I'll just bet you did."

"It wasn't as hard on me as it was on the guys who had a wife and kids at home. I don't know how they did it."

She shouldn't pry. Really, she shouldn't. "You didn't leave anybody behind?" she asked, losing the internal battle quickly.

"Nobody special," he said.

She should let it go. "What's that they say about sailors? A girl in every port?"

"Maybe not *every* port," he said, laughing. "I was a lot of places."

She bet he'd broken his share of hearts.

"You look tired," he said gently. "Why don't you go take a nap?"

"I need to watch this," she said, waving a hand in the direction of the kitchen.

"I got this," he said. "I'll pull it out in exactly forty-five minutes. I promise, I won't forget."

He was right about her being tired. While she'd gotten some sleep the night before, her body felt fatigued, as if she'd been running on empty for a long time.

"Thank you," she said.

"No problem. If you're real lucky, there will be some left when you get up."

She hoped so. Her appetite seemed to be coming back. She no longer felt ill, which was a huge relief.

She walked upstairs, kicked her boots off and lay down. She should sleep when she could. She could see herself, hands on her hips, smiling at someone. *First rule, sleep when you can.*

That had her practically jackknifing in the bed. First rule of what? And who the hell was she talking to?

She took a deep breath, then another. Think, she told herself. Reason it out. What had she been wearing? Blue pants. A lighter blue button-down shirt, tucked in. Tennis shoes.

She stared at her bare feet. She didn't wear tennis shoes. She was sure of that. And the blue pants and shirt had been plain, almost ugly. She liked herself in the pretty linen dress better.

She'd been giving advice. Lightheartedly. But still, she was in a position to offer advice.

She tried to envision the room that she'd been in. Gold wall behind her. Some kind of wallpaper. That was all she could visualize.

She lay back on the bed, all thoughts of a nap gone. Things were coming back. They were. She just hoped it was in time. She hadn't said anything more to Cal but every time she thought of Saturday, she started to feel ill.

She pretended to sleep for an hour before she got up and walked downstairs. She saw a ladder at the bottom of the steps. That was new.

She found Cal in the kitchen. He had indeed pulled the cobbler out. It was nicely browned and there was a large square missing.

"Hi," he said. "Did you sleep?"

"Some," she lied. "What's the ladder for?"

"If the opportunity presents itself, I may tackle the painting while we're here. The ceilings are pretty high upstairs. I'll need a ladder for sure."

"That will be a nice surprise for your brother."

"Trust me on this," he said, "it's the least I can do."

She heard something in his tone, something that didn't quite match the carefree phrase. It was the same thing she heard every time he talked about his brother. Anger. Maybe. Hurt. Possibly. Sorrow. Certainly sounded like it. A myriad of emotions. But whatever it was, he was still lucky.

What she would have given to have her sister back.

Her knees buckled and Cal caught her before she hit the floor. "What the hell?" he said.

She ran a shaky hand through her hair. "I had a sister.

She died when I was seven. She was five years older. I can see her."

He led her from the kitchen to the living room and sat her down on the couch. He crowded in next to her. Then he rubbed her back. Gently. "What's her name?" he asked.

"Mia. I called her My Mia. She was my everything." She could feel hot tears run down her face.

He gathered her into his arms. "What's Mia's last name?" he asked, his lips close to her ear.

"Mia...." She closed her eyes. Damn. Why wouldn't it come? "I don't know," she said.

"It's okay," he said. "How did she die?"

"I can see her. She's running down the stairs, her backpack hanging off one shoulder. She's late."

"For?"

"I don't know."

"Maybe a car accident?"

She shook her head. "She was only five years older. If I was seven, then she was twelve. Too young to drive."

"Someone else could have been driving. One of your parents."

How horrible that would be. But that didn't seem right. "I can remember my parents coming home, walking in the door together and telling me that Mia was dead. My grandmother was there and she was crying."

"Did your grandmother live with you?"

"I don't know."

"What was her name?"

She stared at her hands. She could see herself as a seven year old. Sitting at a table while her grand-

mother stood at the counter, making bread. "Nana."
She looked up.

He was looking at her with such gentle concern that
the dam, the fragile dam that she'd constructed to hold
back her tears, her emotions, her ice-cold fear, dissolved
and she sobbed.

She sobbed for the sister she could not remember.
She sobbed for all the other things that were out of her
reach. She sobbed for the woman who had been wearing a wedding dress and nothing else in the middle of
a snowstorm. She sobbed because she didn't know if it
was ever going to be better.

He pulled her into his chest. Stroked her hair. Rocked
her. Absorbed her grief. Gave her his strength in return.

And when she couldn't cry any more, she stopped.
She felt absolutely empty.

She pulled back and he let her go. She sank back
against the couch cushions. "I'm sorry," she said.

"Don't be," he said. "You've probably been saving
that up for a while."

"I hope the bank is empty," she said, hiccuping once.

He smiled. "Can I get you anything? Water? Coffee?"

"Maybe some water," she said.

He got up and she took advantage of the moment to
pull herself together. He certainly hadn't signed up to
have a hysterical woman on his hands.

When he came back with a glass, her hands were
almost steady. "I'll be fine," she said, assuring both
of them.

He nodded, looking thoughtful. After a minute he
asked, "Want some cobbler?"

She laughed. "Maybe later." She licked her lips. "It's

hard," she admitted. "To just wait. Not knowing if it's ever really going to happen."

"It's only been a little more than a day," he reminded her.

"It seems much longer," she said. "I guess it's like watching water, waiting for it to boil." She looked around the room. "You know what would be helpful right now?"

"Name it," he said.

"A paintbrush?"

"Huh?"

"Can I help you paint? I need something to do. I am going to go crazy just sitting around waiting for my memory to suddenly return."

"You should probably be resting. Letting your mind totally shut down."

"I can't sleep," she said. "Please."

He studied her. "I don't like to trim. How do you feel about that?"

"I'm taking the 'glass is half-full' route. I'll just tell myself that I love it. How will I know the difference?"

"There is that."

HE DECIDED TO start painting in Bray's room. He didn't bother with drop cloths. The carpet was old and would no doubt need to be replaced before they put it on the market.

He had found a stir stick, a paint tray and several brushes in the bathroom attached to Brick's bedroom. He picked up the can of paint and looked at the color.

"Summer Burst," he said. "What kind of color is that?"

"It sounds lovely," Stormy said.

He pried the lid up, gave the paint a stir and said, "Green."

She peered over his shoulder. "It's not green. Green is in-your-face, like it or not. This is lovely. It's soft sage with a hint of violet-blue undertones."

"That's what I said. Green. What's wrong with good old-fashioned white?"

She rolled her eyes and picked up a roll of masking tape. "White? I guess they didn't have HGTV where you were."

He feigned shock. "I know desert chic. Khaki and sand are the new neutrals."

"And Kevlar is all the rage," she added. "Don't be gauche and leave home without it."

"A gentleman is never gauche," he said. He picked up a roller. She was being a good sport but it pained him to see the traces of tears on her cheeks. She'd lost her sister. *My Mia.* That sort of told the whole story.

While it was a tragedy, it was also their first solid clue as to her identity and that was important. Especially when instinct was telling him that she was still in danger. The Mercedes Men had come back to the hotel and had been persistent enough to attempt to look in the warehouse. Cal regretted that the company truck had come along. He wanted to force the altercation with the Mercedes Men, to once and for all figure out why they were in hot pursuit of Stormy. But he certainly hadn't been willing to do that when there was a great likelihood that innocent bystanders would get hurt.

Over the next several hours, they worked in companionable silence. She slipped out of the room several times after hastily explaining that she was working up an appetite and she probably should throw something together for a late dinner.

"Something" ended up being medium-rare roast beef with potatoes and carrots. It was delicious. When he carried his plate over to the sink after dinner, he was amused to see the careful list she was keeping of all the food that she'd removed from the cupboards, the refrigerator and the freezer. One roast, 3.5 pounds. Four potatoes. The list went on.

He walked into the living room and stood at the window. He'd been right about the roads. A plow had come through around eight, which meant that the primary roads were clear or close to it, otherwise the secondary roads would not have received any attention.

The Mercedes Men would make better time now. Would they have thought to take down license plates at the hotels? He thought so. It was basic and what else were the guys in the second car doing while Dumb and Dumber were asking the questions.

Unfortunately, because he'd been out of the country for the better part of the past eight years, he'd never taken the time to establish a residence or update his driver's license. So, when the rental company had asked to see his license and then asked if the address in Ravesville was his current address, he'd taken the easy way out and said yes.

That might come to bite him in the ass but it couldn't be helped now.

If he and Stormy were lucky, there'd be other names that would get checked first.

His cell phone buzzed and he pulled it out of his pocket. "Hi Chase," he said.

"I just wanted to make sure that you'd gotten inside and that everything was okay," Chase said.

"Everything's good," Cal said. "I had a couple free hours so I started painting in Bray's room. I figured that might help get the house ready to sell faster."

"Was that the Summer Burst? How's that look?"

Cal started to say that it was a lovely soft sage with a hint of violet-blue undertones but stopped. His brother would call 911, thinking the paint fumes had gotten to him. "It's good."

"About the house," Chase said, his tone hesitant.

"Yeah?"

"I want it. I want to buy out yours and Bray's shares. I want it for Raney and me."

Cal didn't think there was much in the world that could surprise him but this had. "Of course," he said. "I never figured you'd want it." He laughed. "I'll paint more carefully, make sure I don't get any on the woodwork."

"You do that. Thanks, Cal."

After Chase hung up, Cal continued to stand at the window. Chase was coming back to stay. Wow.

The fifth stair squeaked when Stormy hit it. "Did I hear you on the telephone?"

"Yeah. Talking to Chase. He wants to buy Bray and me out. He wants the house."

"How do you feel about that?"

"I think it's great. He sounds happy. Settled."

"That would be a nice feeling," she said. She didn't sound as if she was whining, just stating a fact. "I'm tired," she said. "I think it's an early bedtime for me."

"Good night," he said. "Thanks again for dinner. It was great."

She smiled and went back upstairs. He sat down on the couch, reached for the book that was in his duffel bag and read for an hour before finally admitting that the book, a biography of Teddy Roosevelt, wasn't holding his attention. He put it down, stretched out, which meant that his feet were hanging off the couch, and closed his eyes.

He didn't wake up until he heard the squeak of the fifth step. Immediately on full alert, he sorted through the possibilities, assessing the danger. His body told him that he'd been asleep for roughly four hours. He breathed in the air. No temperature change to indicate that a door or window had been breached. There'd been no other unexpected noises.

It had to be Stormy. Was she trying to sneak out?

He rolled over, blinked several times to let his eyes adjust to the dark and slowly sat up.

She was poised on the stairs. Enough moonlight shone through the big living room windows that he could see that her long dark hair was wild around her face, making her look both very vulnerable and very alluring. She was once again wearing his sweatpants and T-shirt.

"It's a little early for breakfast," he said.

"I have to tell you something. And it couldn't wait until morning."

Chapter Ten

His heart was beating fast. He knew it wasn't from getting awakened from a sound sleep. No, it was Stormy, in his house, becoming a bigger and bigger part of his life, that was making it speed up.

He stood up. "Have a seat."

"I remembered how I got into the snowdrift."

He wasn't sure he wanted to know. But still, he motioned again for her to sit on the couch. She looked too frail, like a good breeze might blow her down the rest of the stairs.

She sat, with her back against the pillow he'd been using and her legs bent at the knees. He tossed her his blanket.

"Let's share," she said, holding out a portion. "It's chilly."

He sat back down, a full foot away from her toes. He let the blanket fall across his lap. "I'm listening."

"I was in the trunk of a car," she said, her voice emotionless. "I must have been sleeping or knocked out or something because I woke up, feeling sick to my stomach. The car was stopped and I could hear some noise around me but not voices. I knew I had to get out. My hands were tied but I...I'm pretty flexible and was able to turn my body enough and get my arms in a position where I could reach the emergency trunk release. They should have disabled it," she added, shaking her head.

He felt a hot burn in his stomach. She'd been bound and stuffed into the trunk of a car. She could have easily died. They'd probably drugged her, which was why she woke up feeling sick. It was her lucky day that the Mercedes Men had underestimated how long she'd be passed out or that she'd be able to engage the release with her hands tied.

"I got out of the trunk. I was wearing the wedding dress." She said it as if it still surprised her.

"Where were you?"

"A parking lot. Some cars. Lots of semis. It took me a minute to realize it was a truck stop. There was a gas station and a little diner."

"Dawson's Diner, I suspect. You remember the apple pie you had for breakfast yesterday? I got it at that same diner."

She let out a sigh. "I wish I'd known that you were inside. It would have made things so much easier."

"I think we might have just missed each other. The waitress who served me mentioned that right before I'd arrived, there'd been some commotion in the parking lot. It had quieted down fast when two state troopers happened by for afternoon pie."

She thought about that. "They probably did go a little crazy when they came back outside and I was gone. I wasn't there to see it."

"Where exactly did you go?" He held up a finger. "Wait. First tell me if the car you climbed out of was a black Mercedes."

"It was."

He'd assumed so but he'd been trained to not make assumptions. "Okay. Now tell me how you managed to disappear."

"As I said, I was feeling really sick and it was hard to think. But I knew that I needed to get away. I assumed the people who had put me in the trunk were inside the diner. I wasn't going there. I saw a semi that was open in the back and I was going to climb inside. But then I couldn't do it. I couldn't willingly put myself inside another dark space."

He nodded. He understood.

"Then I saw the second truck. It was a big horse trailer, probably one that could carry fifteen or twenty horses. It had horizontal slats. I knew if I could get up onto the side and get my hands and feet into the slats, that I'd have a chance to hang on."

It was a crazy idea but he liked it. And based on the little he knew about Stormy, it seemed to fit her character. And the lack of interest in another dark space was totally understandable. He'd been pinned in a cave for three days once by enemy fire and it had taken him a while before he could even tolerate a dark room.

"I kicked off my shoes. I had these little heels on and I knew that I would be able to grip better with my bare feet."

"It was cold."

"I know. But I figured that was the least of my problems. I wasn't going to die of the cold, at least not for a while. I wanted away from that parking lot, from that horrible trunk. I got lucky. I wasn't hanging on to the outside of it for more than five minutes before the driver came out. I couldn't see his face because he was all bundled up in a hat with earmuffs and a big coat.

He started the vehicle and when I could feel it vibrating under me, I suddenly realized how precarious my situation was. But before I could come up with an alternate plan, he was pulling out of the lot."

"It's amazing that you were able to do this without anybody seeing you."

"The car I'd been in was parked toward the back of the lot. So was the horse trailer. If somebody had been watching, they'd have probably seen me but it was snowing heavily and the wind was blowing. I guess it was lucky that I had on that awful dress. I blended in."

Awful dress. The irony was not lost on him. They both hated that dress. He understood his reasons just fine. And this glimpse of a memory helped him better understand her reaction. She'd been locked in a trunk. That was certainly not the way the happy bride got to the church.

Or back from the church. That was certainly a possible reality. "Do you remember anything from before you were put in the trunk of the car?"

She shook her head. "No."

"Okay. What happened after the truck driver started his rig?"

"I remember being so frightened that he was going to see me clinging to the side of his truck and stop the vehicle. But he either wasn't a very careful driver or his mirrors weren't adjusted at the right angle to see the back of his truck. For whatever reason, he didn't stop and I simply hung on. I was doing pretty well even though it was much colder when we were moving. We took the exit off the highway and went around the corner. The back end of the truck slipped on the slick road. I should have been expecting it but I wasn't prepared. I remembered losing my grip and flying...flying through the air."

She took a deep breath and let it out slowly. "I must have screamed. At least in my dream, I was screaming. That's when I woke up."

He considered the explanation. The room was very quiet. The only sound he could hear was the wind blowing and a stray branch from the tree scratching the back side of the house. "Is it possible that any of it was just a dream, that it didn't really happen?"

She shook her head. "I don't think so. I was dreaming, yes. But my mind was reliving what had occurred. I know it."

"Then I think we need to go back to the truck stop, back to where it started."

Now her breath was coming fast. "I want to do that. I do."

"It might be a dead end," he warned her, his tone serious.

"It might be the answer to everything," she countered. She wanted him to understand that she could handle either outcome, that she wasn't going to fall apart regardless. "At the very least, we can score some truly excellent apple pie."

"Well, I was happy enough with that until I tasted your cobbler."

She blushed. He was glad that he'd been able to tease her. He didn't ever want to see her cry again. "We'll go as soon as we both get up." He stood. He didn't want her to leave. Knew that she should. "You should probably get back to bed."

She hesitated and he almost offered to share the couch.

Then she slowly moved. "It seems as if in bed is the only time my mind is relaxed enough to remember anything."

It wouldn't be right of him to try to convince her to let him hold her through the night. "Your memory is coming," he said. "Be ready," he added.

"Is that some form of *be careful what you wish for*?"

He knew what he was wishing for. And now that he knew that even if she was married, it had been under duress, that should have cleared the path. But she was still bewildered, definitely off her game. He needed to keep himself in check and not add to the stresses in her life.

"Something like that," he said. "Good night, Stormy."

He watched her walk up the stairs. Then he held the portion of the quilt that had covered her close to his face, breathing deep. He didn't close his own eyes again for a very long time.

SHE WAS AWAKE well before dawn but she stayed in bed. It was warm and she wasn't quite ready to face Cal yet. Something had happened between the two of them as they'd huddled in the darkness, sharing the quilt.

He hadn't touched her and unlike at the toboggan factory, she'd managed to keep her fingers and her lips to herself. But still, there had been a connection. It had comforted, warmed, while at the same time, it had brought her to the edge of her control.

That was why she'd gone quietly upstairs when he'd suggested it. Because she'd known that he was trying to do the right thing, trying to keep things from getting more complicated.

She was a guest in his home. He deserved that she'd at least try to leave it *and him* unscathed.

Perhaps if the memory of waking up in the trunk of the car had come to her in the daytime, it might have been different. Maybe she'd have been able to process it alone. But in the middle of the night, she'd needed someone else. On her way down the stairs, she'd deliberately stepped on the fifth step, knowing that it would loudly creak. It was her way of announcing that she was coming.

Her way of giving him the opportunity to decide how he wanted to play it. If he continued to lie on the couch, pretending to still be asleep, she would have gotten a glass of water from the kitchen and returned upstairs, as if that had been her whole mission.

But he'd rolled over, invited her to share his couch and listened. And she'd been very grateful. She'd needed to talk about what she'd remembered. When she'd told him about being locked in the trunk, she could feel his anger. He'd seemed almost amused by the fact that she'd chosen to hang on to the side of a truck in the middle of a blizzard. Even now, she thought she'd likely done the right thing. It had gotten her away from the men, even if getting tossed from the truck and hitting her head had caused a whole lot of other problems.

Between what she remembered about the ghost and the wedding dress and now this, knowing that she'd been locked in the truck of a car, was proof positive that she hadn't been the happy bride-to-be. She knew that Cal had been bothered by the wedding dress and what it meant. It hadn't been the same for her. She'd *known* that it was nothing. Still, it had been a bit hard to ignore.

Yesterday, when she'd remembered her silver ring,

it had given her a reason to pause. Something told her that silver ring was very important to her. Was it a wedding ring? An engagement ring? She could see it clearly and it didn't look like that but maybe the giver had been unconventional. It looked old. Maybe it was a family heirloom?

When she thought about her ring, her body seemed to have a reaction. She felt hot and slightly nauseous and very angry. It was just crazy.

Cal had said, *Your memory is coming. Be ready.* Was she? Or had something so horrible happened that she was blocking it out. Maybe it had nothing to do with the bump on her head? Maybe it was simply her way of coping.

She needed to get over it.

They would go to the truck stop today. She would stand in the parking lot, breathe in the cold air and will her memory to return. She swung her legs over the side of the bed.

Once she finished a quick shower and dried her hair, she dug into the closet for some additional clothes. She found a pair of black leggings and a long red sweater. She pulled on the black boots that were a little big but a huge step up from going barefoot. She looked at the knife that Cal had given her the day before. She slipped it into the pocket of the red sweater.

When she walked downstairs, Cal was standing in the kitchen, his rear end resting against the counter, drinking a cup of coffee. He looked fresh and capable and once again, she thanked her good luck that he'd been the one who'd found her in the snowdrift. "Good morning," she said.

"I'd make you some toast with your coffee but there's no bread."

"Maybe we can actually get breakfast at the diner," she said.

"The cook, or I should say chef, is a good one. We go for information, maybe get an omelet as the icing on the cake."

She shook her head. "Based on the apple pie, I'd rather have the cake."

He drained his coffee. "Let's go." He picked up his coat and under it was another black wool jacket. "I got this out of the closet upstairs. It belonged to my mom. Will it work?"

"Perfect," she said.

The road in front of the house was still snow-covered but once they got back to the highway, it was much better. They drove through Ravesville, dutifully obeying all the four-way stops. Cal accelerated as they left town. It was definitely better driving. Easier for them and easier for the men chasing her.

Almost as if he'd read her mind, Cal turned to look at her. "Nervous?"

She shook her head. "Anxious. Hopeful." She turned to stare out the window. Out of the corner of her eye, she saw him turn on the car radio.

She didn't want to listen to talk radio. She wanted to know more about Cal. "Will you stay in Missouri?" she asked. "After your visit with your brothers?"

"I don't know. I haven't thought much about it."

"You don't have a job to go back to?"

"Nope. Gave them my notice. I've been thinking about starting up a small engineering company, taking on projects that really interest me. Maybe contract

with the government on building ships and submarines.
Every time I was on one, I'd find all kinds of things
that could have been designed better, more efficiently,
so that it would work better. I think I'd find that worthwhile, making sure the next generation of sailors has
it better."

"That sounds very cool," she said. "You could probably do that work from anywhere."

He shrugged. "Maybe I should buy the Fitzler property, live just down the road from my old house."

He was joking. But the idea didn't seem all that crazy
to her. "It has that big outbuilding," she said. "Certainly
big enough for creating prototypes or whatever it is you
engineering types like to make."

He scratched his head. "You know what they say, you
can never go back home again. Somebody very wise
probably learned that the hard way."

"That's just something that parents try to tell their
kids when they're graduating from college. Come on.
It would be cool. You'd be in one house and Chase in
the other. It would be as if you owned the road. Like the
road might really be called Route 6 but everyone in the
community would refer to as Hollister Road."

"Now you're getting crazy," he said good-naturedly.

She let it go. It was his decision. She would be long
gone. With that unsettling thought heavy on her heart,
she reached for the radio knob and started looking for
something to listen to.

They didn't talk again until Cal said, "Five minutes out."

She rubbed her hands together in anticipation.

"It's possible that the Mercedes Men may have the
location staked out," he said.

She'd thought of that. The risk was worth it. For some reason, the Mercedes Men had stopped at Dawson's Diner. She didn't think it was as simple as they suddenly had a hankering for a ham sandwich. "I'll get down on the floor. You check out the parking lot. If we see their cars, we leave."

"That should work."

She unbuckled her seat belt and got on the floor. "I hope they're there," she said.

He chuckled. "Ready to bust somebody's chops?"

"Maybe."

"Even if the lot is clear, I should probably go in first, just to make sure that they haven't gotten smart and changed vehicles. Give me a three-minute head start."

She could tell when they turned into the lot. It was rougher and Cal slowed way down. The SUV made a big circle. He was going around the building. "Anything?" she asked.

"Nope. I'm going to park. Three minutes," he reminded her.

"Got it," she said.

He parked, shut off the vehicle and got out without another word. She looked at her watch.

The first minute went fast. The next sixty seconds dragged on. She held her breath for the third minute. Then she straightened up, opened her door and calmly walked into the diner.

Cal was sitting in a booth and smiled at her. She sat down.

He pushed a menu in her direction. "See anybody interesting?" he asked, his voice low.

She shook her head. As she'd walked in, she'd looked at everybody. There hadn't been a flicker of recognition in her blank slate of a mind and nothing alarming on anyone else's faces.

"The same waitress is working today. Her name is Lena. Maybe she'll be helpful. I left a really good tip."

Despite her anxiety, she smiled. When the waitress came up, she was wearing a bright fuchsia smock and white pants and her hair was pulled up into a lopsided bun. She was probably midforties.

"Hey," Lena said, looking at Cal. "I remember you."

A woman would have to be dead not to remember Cal Hollister. Big tip or not.

He smiled up at her. "The apple pie was so good I had to come back."

"Glad the storm didn't get you," Lena said. She turned toward Stormy. "Can I get you some…" Her voice trailed off. "Coffee?" Lena finished stronger.

She had to take the chance. "Have we met?" she asked. "You look so familiar." She did her best *I'm sweet and harmless* imitation.

"I…uh…" Lena stammered and looked at Cal. He had a relaxed look on his face and was looking at the menu as if his greatest ambition in life was to discover the morning breakfast special.

"I don't think we've met," Lena said. "But I saw a picture of you. Just the other day."

"Oh really, which one was that?"

"You were sitting at a bar. Wearing a royal blue dress that crossed in the front."

She could see the dress. Could see herself at the bar. She'd been nursing a glass of white wine. Waiting.

Damn it. Who was she waiting for?

Who the hell had taken a picture of her there?

And how in the world had this woman seen it? "Love that dress," she said.

"Your fiancé was flashing it around when he came in to talk to Pietro about the food for your wedding reception. He's pretty proud of you."

She was glad no one had yet poured her coffee. She would have surely choked on it. She couldn't very well ask her fiancé's name or for a description. She put a finger up to her lips and tapped thoughtfully. "I'm trying to remember how he knew Pietro," she said.

"He told me that the two of them had worked together at Moldaire College. I got the impression that they hadn't seen each other for a while." Lena lowered her voice. "I know Pietro and his wife moved here about four years ago. Unfortunately for him, she and their son left about a year ago, moved back to Kansas City. He stayed, though, said he liked the area."

"That all rings a bell," she said. "You know, I'd love to say hello to Pietro. Is he working today?"

"Nope. It's his day off."

"Shoot." She waved her hand in Cal's direction. "My stepbrother helped me pay for the wedding. We'd both appreciate having the opportunity to thank Pietro personally for making it such a special day. Does he live nearby?"

"A couple miles down on Summerfield Road," Lena said. "Big yellow house on the hill."

Cal gave an almost imperceptible nod.

"Great," she said.

Lena smiled. "He's a nice guy but his ego does need to be stroked. He'll enjoy hearing how the food was at the reception."

Her tongue felt too big for her mouth. Just because

he'd fixed food for the wedding reception didn't necessarily mean there'd been a wedding. "Delicious," she said. "It was delicious."

"You two going to have breakfast?" Lena asked.

She could hardly wait to follow up on the two leads. Pietro and Moldaire College. But it would look odd if they didn't eat. "Absolutely. I'll take a short stack of pancakes and a big cup of coffee."

Cal ordered eggs, bacon and hash browns along with coffee. He waited to speak until Lena was at the other end of the restaurant.

"Nicely done," he said.

"Thank you. We probably better leave her another big tip."

Chapter Eleven

Stormy ate half her pancakes before pushing her plate aside. He figured that was as good as he could have hoped for.

He hadn't been exaggerating when he'd told her that she'd done a nice job. She'd struck just the right chord with Lena and the two of them had been chatting like old friends.

Lena came by, dropped off the check and cleared their plates. He took one last swig of coffee. "Ready?"

Stormy nodded.

He saw her glance at the check amount and knew that she was likely going to add it to her list of expenses to reimburse, somewhere between basil and flour.

He left Lena a tip in line with what he'd left the first time. Her information had been golden but there was no sense letting on that they were too grateful.

He led the way out of the diner and, after opening the door, stood in the entrance and scanned the exterior. Nothing too different than when they'd come in. Different vehicles getting gas, of course, but none of them was a black Mercedes. Of course, it was possible that they were being observed from a distance. He and Stormy had done just that at the toboggan factory. He glanced off into the distance. There wasn't anything close enough to warrant concern. He stepped away from the doorstep and started walking. He shortened his stride so that Stormy could easily keep up.

"Pietro or Moldaire College?" he asked.

She opened her door and slid in. He walked around the SUV.

"Pietro," she said, buckling her seat belt. "Even if Moldaire is a small college, it will still be like looking for a needle in a haystack because I won't know where to start."

"The first time I met Lena, she told me that Pietro was a chef at a restaurant in the student union at the college. Catered all the significant events."

"That helps," she said. "Still, let's see if we can find him. Maybe he can start to fill in the missing pieces."

"He might be in on it. Maybe one of the Mercedes Men is his best friend. His brother."

She sat back in her seat, evidently considering his comment. He appreciated that in her excitement at having a lead, she didn't immediately dismiss his concerns. She was a thinker.

"Lena said they worked together at the college. She didn't say they were old friends or any kind of relative."

"Maybe she doesn't know the extent of their relationship," he countered.

"Maybe. I need to take the chance. But you're right. There is a risk. I'm going alone."

"Like hell you are," he said.

"It only makes sense," she argued. "If he's in on it, then we don't want him to know anything about you. If that happens, your home will be compromised."

"What if he tries to detain you until his friends come

back?" He didn't know why he was bothering to even discuss it. It wasn't going to happen.

"Let me see your gun," she said.

That surprised him. "Why?"

"I want to see if it feels familiar."

He didn't care if she'd given shooting instruction to the military. "Do you know how to shoot a gun?"

She shrugged. "I think so."

"The fact that you *think* you know how to shoot a gun is not terribly comforting."

She waved a hand. "I promise I won't shoot myself or him, unnecessarily," she added.

He could feel his breakfast rumble in his stomach. He, who never got nervous about anything. "I'm not giving you my gun." He started the car. Pulled out of the lot.

"I assume you know where Summerfield Road is?"

"Sort of. I think it's only a few miles from where I found you. There won't be that many houses. We should be able to find the yellow one on the hill."

"Okay. Get me close and then I'll let you out. Once I talk to him, I'll be back to get you."

"No. You let me out, give me ten minutes to get into position and then drive up to the house."

She didn't say anything. Then finally she sighed. Loudly. "Fine. Let's just do this."

He took the same exit off the Interstate that he'd taken just two days ago. When he made the sweeping turn, he couldn't help but look at the place where he'd found Stormy. The wind had whipped the snow around and there was no sign that he or anyone else had tromped through the ditch.

"Was that the place?" she asked, her voice soft.

He slowed down. "Yeah. Want to have a closer look?"

She shook her head. "I am amazed that you saw me from the road. I…could have easily frozen to death."

She could have. That thought made his knees feel as if they were made of jelly. But she didn't need to be dwelling on the what-ifs. "I think you were probably knocked out when you hit your head on the fence post. You were just regaining consciousness when I arrived. I suspect you'd have gotten up and thumbed a ride from the next car."

"I'm not sure," she admitted.

She was quiet for another two miles before she turned in her seat. "I'm glad it was you," she said. "I'm glad and very, very grateful it was you."

His throat felt tight. He was falling for Stormy. He didn't know her real name or her real story but none of that mattered.

"Did you recall that picture that Lena was describing, the one where you were wearing the blue dress?"

"Oddly enough, I did. I can't remember my own name but I could see myself in the blue dress, sitting at the bar."

"What bar?" he asked casually.

"The Blue Mango." She turned to him wide-eyed.

"Who were you with?" he followed up quickly.

SHE TRIED TO visualize it. But it made her feel sick. She shook her head. "It appears my subconscious is onto your tricks."

"At least we got The Blue Mango," he said. "That first night, in the hotel, you smelled like mangoes."

She felt warm. "It was the hotel lotion."

"I'm fond of mangoes," he said.

She wasn't sure what to say to that. "Have you ever heard of this place?"

"Nope." He pulled his cell phone from his shirt pocket and tossed it into her lap. "See if you can find it."

His browser was fast and it took less than a minute. "There are three Blue Mangoes. One in Connecticut, one in Los Angeles and one in Kansas City."

"Focus on the Kansas City one," he said. "Proximity should never be ignored."

"It's on Lager Avenue. They have their menu posted. It's a restaurant, too, not just a bar. Looks good," she added, rather stupidly, she thought. His remembering how she'd smelled that first night had shaken her.

He slowed down to take the turn off onto Summerfield Road. It was a roughly paved road with large potholes at the edges.

Heck, maybe she'd only remembered The Blue Mango because she'd used mango lotion post injury. She certainly couldn't explain why some things were there and most things were not.

But maybe they wouldn't need The Blue Mango after all. Maybe everything would fall into place after their visit with the chef.

She knew that Cal was worried but she intended to be very careful. The knowledge that she'd been tied and drugged just days ago was still very fresh in her mind. But she'd push the man for answers if she had to. Time was ticking away. It was already Thursday.

Two miles down the road, she saw a yellow house on the hill. "Think that's it?"

"I'm sure it is. I'll do a pass-by first," Cal said.

"Good idea," she said. Cal didn't speed up or slow down as he drove by the two-story farmhouse. There were no cars in the driveway. That didn't mean much. There was a separate two-car garage. Pietro could be parked there. Visitors, too, she supposed.

What was clear was that there had been some activity at the house recently. The driveway was partially cleared of snow, the work of a shovel probably, versus a snowblower. Someone had made a path wide enough for one car that led up to the garage.

She couldn't tell if there were footsteps in the snow leading from the garage to the house but she assumed so. When she got close, she'd be able to tell if it was one set or multiple.

Once they crested the hill and were out of sight of the house, Cal slowed down quickly and stopped the vehicle. "I'll walk from here, through that field, and circle around behind the house. Ten minutes should be plenty."

He was going to be walking in knee-high snow, with waist-high drifts in places. He was going to get soaked. "Are you sure you want to do this?"

"Absolutely." He pulled on his gloves. "If something goes wrong," he said, "your job is to get the hell out of here. Don't worry about me."

"Nothing is going to go wrong."

He turned toward her and before she realized his intent, he'd pulled her toward him. He kissed her hard. It was fast, intense and made her want more. "You got that right," he said and opened his door.

If she'd thought it was difficult to wait three minutes before going into the diner, ten minutes was an eternity. In the entire time, no cars came from either direction. That was good in that there was no one to see Cal sprinting across the field.

She couldn't believe the man was running through

the snow. He was clearly in amazing shape. It would have been quicksand to her but he was acting like it was warm surf.

At seven minutes he was too far away to distinguish from the trees that ran the perimeter of Pietro's property. At exactly ten minutes, she put the car into Drive and took off.

The driveway leading up to the house worried her and something told her that she didn't drive in snow very often. As she made the turn, the back tires lost traction and the rear end swerved. She got the vehicle under control, stayed in the path and drove up to the house.

She did not see Cal but she knew he was there.

She got out, listening carefully. She didn't hear anything unusual. She studied the footprints in the snow. It was hard to tell whether it had been one person making multiple trips between the house and garage or multiple people making one trip. She stepped up onto the porch, looked for a doorbell, didn't see one and started knocking.

About a minute later, the inside door opened. A middle-aged man with dark hair cut short and heavy, black-framed glasses stood beyond the screen door. He was wearing gray sweats and a white T-shirt. That almost made her smile because that was what she'd been wearing when she'd borrowed Cal's clothes. If she hadn't changed, they'd have been twins.

The man was holding a yellow pepper in his hand. That boosted her courage. Men with yellow peppers were harmless. This had to be Pietro, the chef.

He looked around her, as if he was trying to figure out how she'd ended up on his porch. He didn't show any signs of recognizing her but if the Mercedes Men had showed Lena her picture, it was a good hunch that they'd also shown the chef.

"Can I help you?" he asked.

She smiled. "I'm sorry to bother you but you recently catered my wedding and I just wanted to tell you what a wonderful job you did."

There was no change of expression. She started to get very nervous.

"I…uh…got your name from Lena at the diner," she added.

"How was the pork?" he asked.

"Delicious," she said.

"The rosemary potatoes?"

Uh. "Fragrant. Wonderful."

"Good." His tone was flat.

She remembered that Lena had said that he needed his ego stroked. Maybe *delicious* and *wonderful* weren't enough. *Fragrant* probably didn't even count. She should have gone for something more. *Awesome. Best ever. Cooking-show worthy.* "I was wondering if you had a card or something that I could give to my girlfriends. A couple of them are getting married soon."

He scratched his head. "No. Listen, I don't mean to be rude but I'm in the middle of something."

She understood why he'd become a chef and stayed in the kitchen. He didn't have the personality to interact with customers. "But—"

He slammed the door in her face.

She wanted to kick it open and demand more information. But that didn't necessarily seem like the thing to do.

She walked to the SUV and got in. He hadn't cleared

enough of the driveway to pull around, so she had to back down the lane. It allowed her to keep an eye on the house. She still did not see Cal.

She turned, drove over the hill, slowed and stopped. It was almost twelve minutes before she saw Cal coming across the field. Once he got close, she got out of the driver's seat and into the passenger seat. He entered the vehicle in a burst of cold air and pure male.

"Did you hear?" she asked.

"Every word," he said.

"Where the heck were you?" she asked.

"Behind the garbage cans next to the garage. I wanted to see what vehicle was in the garage and then I wanted a position where I had a clear shot at the front door."

He said it without emotion and she knew that had Pietro presented any danger to her, Cal would have stepped in quickly and taken care of things.

"I didn't get anything," she said. "I'm sorry."

"You got something. I don't think Pietro and your groom—"

"He's not *my* groom," she interrupted.

He smiled. "Okay. How about we just call him G for short. I don't think Pietro and G were friends. He pretended not to recognize you but when you mentioned the food, you didn't surprise him. That was plain. And it was smart to try to reel him in with the mention of friends who might need catering. But he was so clearly done with you. That has to mean something. And I think it speaks to his relationship with…ah, you know who."

It struck her that he was being deliberately a little provocative and silly to make her feel better. He had realized that she'd be bitterly disappointed and had wanted to head that off at the pass.

Cal Hollister was a very nice guy.

"Maybe G and his friends have given up looking for me," she said.

"Maybe," he said. They reached the highway. Cal made the required stop. "I stuck around for a few minutes to see if he was going to make any phone calls. He didn't. Just picked up a big knife and attacked the pepper with a vengeance. You coming to his house bothered him. I don't know why. But I think it might be important."

"Should we go back? Should we get the truth out of him?"

"Are you willing to hurt him to do that?"

"I… No. No, I'm not."

"Then I don't think so. It would take some persuasion. Our best bet is to go to Moldaire College. It's just a little east of Kansas City. That's a ninety-minute drive from here. We could check it out. There are also four bridal stores in the area."

"Let's go," she said.

They got back on the Interstate and it was smooth sailing. They didn't talk. Yet the silence was comfortable. She closed her eyes. The next thing she knew he was gently shaking her shoulder. The vehicle was stopped.

"We're here."

She blinked. "I don't know why I can't stay awake."

"Well, there's probably a good reason. Earlier you said that you woke up in the trunk feeling sick. You do realize that you were probably drugged. That takes a toll on the body if it happened repeatedly."

She swallowed hard. "I thought of that," she said.

"That first night in the hotel, in the shower, I... I looked for...signs to see if I'd been raped."

The car started to roll and he slammed his foot on the brake and shoved it into Park. "I should have taken you to the damn hospital," he said, clearly angry with himself.

She reached out and touched his arm. "I wasn't. I know I can't be sure but I really don't think anything like that happened."

"I want to kill them all for making you even have any doubt."

If she hadn't already started to love Cal Hollister, that would have been the push that sent her tumbling down the slide. "Thank you," she said.

He still looked so troubled. "Where to now?" she asked, hoping to get him refocused.

He looked around. They were in a parking lot, surrounded by stone buildings of varying heights but none over four stories. The buildings were solid structures with heavy, arched windows and big doorways. These were buildings that had been here for a long time, probably a hundred years.

"I don't know much about Moldaire," he said. "It's private and very expensive. It was way out of my price range when I was looking at colleges. It's not Ivy League but probably somewhere in the second tier of that group."

"How big?"

"Maybe six to eight thousand students. Liberal arts focus if I remember correctly."

She looked around. There were huge trees, bare of leaves, beautiful with fresh snow clinging to their branches. There were heavily bundled-up students walking fast, their heads down to avoid the cold.

"See anything that rings a bell?" he asked.

There was something but she couldn't put her finger on it. "You said that Pietro was a chef here at the student union. Let's go have lunch there."

"You didn't answer me when I asked if anything rang a bell. Talk to me."

"I have been here before," she said slowly. "I'm not sure when or why but this place is familiar to me. And I think I was here recently."

"Okay. That's exactly why we're not going to the student union. Too big, too many potential casualties if something goes wrong."

"But—"

He shook his head. "We'll drive around the campus. Give you a couple more vantage points. That's the best I'm willing to do today. Maybe this will be enough to trip that little wire in your brain and everything will be clear as mud tomorrow."

"I hope so," she said.

He stopped at four more places around the picturesque campus. Once near the dorms, once by the science building, once down the street from the administration building and once near the student union, which was one of the larger buildings. There was a sign advertising the restaurant inside and a telephone number to contact if someone was interested in renting a room in the Union Hotel, which by the looks of the building were probably the upper floors. Nothing felt more or less familiar. "I'm sorry," she said.

"No problem."

He didn't even sound disappointed and she wanted

to cry. After the encounter with Pietro, she'd had her hopes pinned on this. "We're running out of clues."

"That's the glass half-empty. You might say we're narrowing the possibilities. Half-full."

"Does my glass have alcohol in it?"

"A truly excellent scotch."

She wrinkled her nose. "I don't think I drink scotch."

"Ah, but I do." He picked up his cell phone. Pushed a few buttons. "Let's go dress shopping."

"Four words I never expected to hear Cal Hollister say," she muttered. "Maybe you've already been drinking."

He smiled. "Maybe I love shopping."

"And maybe I love cleaning fish." She paused for effect. "I think we're both lying."

It was a crazy little conversation to be having on a cold day in the middle of the nowhere but it had accomplished exactly what she suspected Cal had intended. There was no time for a pity party. She needed to keep moving forward. The answers were somewhere. She just needed to turn over the right rock.

Chapter Twelve

Jo-Jo's Bridal Boutique was in a strip mall, in between a dry cleaner's and a nail salon. They parked in front and watched for a few minutes. Two women, probably a daughter with her mother, came out of the shop carrying a garment bag. No one went in.

"We should be prepared for the possibility that your picture was flashed around here. If G showed your picture to Lena and Pietro, there's a possibility of that. Sort of a *see my beautiful bride, now give me the perfect dress for her* kind of moment."

"How do we play this?"

"As close to the truth as possible. Our goal is to get information on G and the rest of the Mercedes Men. How about we tell them that you recently got married after your fiancé surprised you with a wedding dress but now you're attempting to resell the dress and you have a buyer who won't pay the price you're asking unless she sees an original invoice?"

"They might not be inclined to want to be helpful. After all, every resold dress is one less new dress they might sell."

"You'll pull it off," he said confidently. He opened his door. "Let's do this."

The store was small and stuffed with mostly white and ivory bridal gowns. On the far wall was an assortment of colored dresses suitable for bridesmaids.

There was one store clerk, a middle-aged woman with her glasses on the far end of her nose. When she greeted them, she looked over the top of her glasses. "Good afternoon. My name is Ann. What can I help you with?"

"Hi. My name is Mary and this is my stepbrother, Tom. I recently got married. My fiancé surprised me with this gorgeous dress." She held out Cal's phone so that the woman could see the picture of the dress and the close-up of the label. "I think he bought it here. It was so sweet. And now I feel terrible but I don't want him to know about some of my credit card bills. I need to get them paid off before the next statement comes. I'm hoping to resell my dress and I've got a buyer but she won't pay the price I'm asking unless she sees the original receipt. I can't ask my husband," she finished.

Ann pushed her glasses up and took another long look at the picture. Then she walked over to one of the racks and flipped through the long dresses. Finally, she turned. "I wish I could help. We sell that designer but not that particular dress. I don't think he bought it here."

She bit back her disappointment. "Oh, I'm so sorry to have bothered you, then. You don't happen to have any idea where he might have gotten it?"

"You might try the Dream a Little Dream on Cleveland Avenue. They're our biggest competitor."

She recognized the store name from the list she and Cal had created. "Thank you so much," she said.

She and Cal walked back to the SUV. He started the

car and pulled out of the parking lot. "Nicely done. You took my story and made it better."

It had been effortless and it made her think that she was accustomed to doing things like this. "I think I must be an accountant. Lying doesn't seem to bother me."

He laughed. "Figures lie and liars figure."

She looked at his phone. "How far away is Cleveland Avenue?"

"We'll be there in fifteen minutes."

They had to wait for a train so it took them seventeen minutes. The two-story store was on the corner of a busy intersection. The area was more commercial and more upscale. There was an art studio next door and a big bank across the street.

They parked and went inside. There were several salesclerks, all helping customers. She and Cal pretended to look around until another salesclerk walked out of the back room.

"Can I help you?" the girl asked. She was young, maybe not even twenty, and she wore a very short skirt.

"I'm Mary and this is my stepbrother, Tom," she said, launching into her story. When she got to the part about the credit card debt, the salesclerk nodded, as if she understood that particular predicament.

"I was here that day," the salesclerk said. "I wasn't waiting on your fiancé but I did see your picture. He was showing it to everyone."

Just like Cal had thought. "It's embarrassing," she said, rolling her eyes.

The girl laughed. "We all thought it was cute but we weren't sure when he said he was going to surprise you with the dress. Most of our brides like to pick out their own dresses. I know I'd want to."

"It was a lovely gown." She gritted her teeth.

"One of my favorites. And that's saying something since we have over 200 different styles. You must have had a real spur-of-the-moment wedding."

"Because…." She let her voice trail off.

"Because hardly anyone wants to buy a gown right off the floor," the salesclerk said. "They want to order a new gown, one that hasn't been tried on by other customers. But when we told your fiancé that was how it generally worked, he said that he had to have the one off the rack."

"It was really sweet of him to take care of it. That's why I feel awful now. But do you think you'd have the original invoice? Maybe if I could just take a quick cell phone picture of it so that I could send it to the buyer."

The girl scratched her head. "We might have it back in the office." She glanced around the store. "I guess everyone else has been waited on."

"I know that I'm taking you off the sales floor and you probably work on commission. I'll make it worth your while." It was just one more thing to add to the list of items that she needed to repay.

"I appreciate that," said the salesclerk. "I'll just be a few minutes."

Without having to ask him, Cal stuffed a fifty-dollar bill into her hand before moving toward the front of the store and taking a spot near the cash register, where he could keep watch on both the store and the parking lot.

She wandered around the store, casually looking at the various dresses. She was on her second cursory lap when she saw a dress that made her stop. It was ivory. A smooth satin. Off the shoulders and fitted through the hips, it gently flared at the knees with a swirl of the skirt. Stunning. There was no other word.

She couldn't help herself. She lifted the hanger off the rack, walked over to the mirror and held the dress up to her body.

An older woman, knitting while she waited, looked up. "That's lovely dear. My granddaughter should look at that one."

She smiled and took another quick glance in the mirror. Out of the corner of her eye, she saw that Cal was watching her. Embarrassed, she hurriedly stuffed the dress back onto the crowded rack.

It took the salesclerk another five minutes. Finally she came out of the back room holding an invoice. "Found it," she said. The girl held out a yellow five-by-eight receipt, the kind that gets torn off a book of receipts.

She reached for it and willed her hands not to shake. She realized that Cal had very quickly and quietly come to stand next to her.

Next to customer name, some earnest salesclerk had written Golya Paladis. Next to address was written Moldaire College. The dress had cost fourteen hundred dollars.

"That's odd," said the salesclerk.

"What?" she asked. Her head was whirling. *Golya Paladis*. Did the name mean anything to her?

"We're supposed to get an address and a contact number," the girl said. "But maybe because we weren't ordering the dress that wasn't necessary."

She pointed to a small circle with an X inside. "What does this mean?"

The salesclerk smiled. "That he paid cash. The very best kind of sale."

She pulled out Cal's cell phone. "May I?" she said at the same time she discreetly pushed the fifty-dollar bill in the salesclerk's direction.

"I don't see why not. It's your dress," the girl said.

She took the picture, thanked the girl again, and she and Cal left the store. Back in the SUV, neither of them said anything for a minute.

"Golya Paladis," Cal said. "When we called him G, we were right all along."

She rolled her eyes.

"Mean anything to you?" Cal asked.

"Not at the moment," she said. "Maybe you could kick me in the head, knock everything loose and that would all change."

"That'll be our backup plan. Let's see if we can find out a little more about him." He started punching info into his smartphone. After a few minutes, he frowned and shook his head. "I don't like this."

"Now what?" she asked.

"There's nothing. And I have access to some sites that not everyone would have because of my work as an independent contractor and even those are coming up empty."

"It's an alias."

"Probably. But Golya—"

"Let's just keep calling him G. I don't really want to think of him as a real person. He's shallow, worthy of only an initial."

"Okay. G bought the dress on Sunday. Two days before the wedding. That was the same day that Lena at the diner said that he contacted Pietro. Remember that she said Pietro was upset and she assumed it was because he had very little notice to get food ready for the reception."

"So I somehow fell into his hands before that."

"Yes. And I don't think too far in advance of that. He seemed to be moving fairly quickly, like his plan was coming together very fast. I think it's possible that you fell into his hands, that perhaps marrying you was an impulse that wasn't well thought out. Like you said earlier, what would have made him think that he could keep you once you were no longer drugged?"

"Maybe he'd been stalking me. He had a picture of me. I remember the picture. I remember sitting at the bar at The Blue Mango. I was having fun. It had to be before G. But maybe he was there. Watching."

She couldn't control the involuntary shudder.

"Doesn't matter how he got it. It's helped us. People remember you and they trust our story," he added with his usual optimism.

"Half-full?" she said.

"Always." He pulled out of the lot. "What do you want to do? We could go home or we could try The Blue Mango. Your decision."

She was exhausted. As Cal had suggested, she suspected that she was still feeling the effects of the drugs in her system. Plus it had already been a day of ups and downs, starting with the visit to Pietro's, the trip to Moldaire that had left her unsettled but no wiser and now this, a success to find out the full name of one of the Mercedes Men, only to discover that he didn't really exist.

She had to keep going. "The Blue Mango."

It took them forty minutes to find the place. It was

in a section of Kansas City that had become gentrified within the past twenty years and cute little businesses were springing up in the hundred-year-old shopping district. The Blue Mango was on the corner, a two-story brick building that appeared to be an apartment on top, restaurant/bar on the bottom.

There were no lights on in the building and many empty parking places nearby.

She looked at her watch. It was just before four. "It says on the website that they're open for lunch and dinner. It doesn't say anything about them closing in between."

"There's a note on the front door," Cal said. "Wait here while I go read it."

He was back in the SUV in less than a minute. "It's handwritten, apologizing for being unexpectedly closed today. They will reopen tomorrow at normal time."

She rubbed her head. "Do you think that their being closed has anything to do with me?"

"I don't know. It's a nice place. Doesn't look like the type that posts a handwritten note on the door."

"I'm going to call them," she said. "It doesn't look like anyone is inside but maybe the number is to someone's cell phone. Maybe we can get some information." She needed to keep pushing. She felt it.

He handed her his phone. She found the website and dialed the number. It rang and rang. Finally, she hung up.

"Now what?" she asked.

"Let's go home," he said. They were sixty miles down the road when he turned to her. "I'm going to get gas. I think you better get out of view. There's no telling how many resources they have and how many places they're watching. Once I fill the tank, I'll go into the grocery mart inside. I can probably get milk, bread and eggs. The basics."

She understood what he wasn't saying. There were probably a number of grocery stores in the small towns surrounding the Interstate but he wasn't taking a chance that the Mercedes Men hadn't effectively spread the word in the small communities to look for someone like her. "I should cut my hair. Dye it blond."

He shook his head. "Not yet," he said, his eyes amused. "I like your hair. It feels like silk."

That was nice. A little flustered, she hurried to un-buckle her seat belt and get on the floor so that her head would not show above the windows.

She felt him slow, then turn, then slow some more. She sensed that he was probably driving around the gas station before pulling into one of the bays. "How's it look?" she said.

"Nothing unusual," he said. He stopped the car, got out, and soon she could hear the sounds of fuel pouring into the vehicle. She would need to add gas to the list of items to reimburse him for.

The mileage reimbursement rate was 57.5 cents a mile.

She jerked up, almost forgetting that she was supposed to hide. She could remember having a conversation about the mileage rate recently. She'd been laughing. She could see herself. Sitting in a chair, in front of a plain table, a laptop computer in front of her. She was pointing at a screen. "Just use the form," she said. "It's online."

She'd been talking to someone. With someone. Who?

She heard the door open and barely stifled her squeak. Cal swung into the seat. He put the sack of groceries he was carrying on the floor of the backseat. "Everything okay?" he asked, already pulling away.

She waited until he told her she could safely get up before telling him everything. When she finished, she added, "I was kidding before but maybe I really am an accountant."

"You'll be handy to have around at tax time," he said easily. "Tell me about the chair."

The chair. He wanted to hear about the chair. But she realized that he was asking about exactly what she'd been trying to work through in her head—the details.

"Blond wood. With arms. Padded seat. Some kind of mauve print."

"Hotel issue?" he asked.

She nodded. "Maybe."

"What were you wearing?"

The very same thing that she'd been wearing in the one other brief vision that she'd had. But she'd never mentioned that one to him and didn't think it was prudent to do so now. She didn't want him to think she was hiding things. "Blue button-down shirt. Tucked in. Blue pants. Not blue jeans. Maybe khaki." She hadn't been able to see her shoes. But the other time, she'd distinctly seen that she was wearing tennis shoes. "White tennis shoes. I had my hair in a ponytail. That seems weird. I feel like it was unusual for me to have my hair like that."

"Anything else about your appearance?"

"No. But there was something next to the laptop. A blue lanyard, attached to a plastic badge. You know the kind. You would use it to clock in or open a door."

"Yours?"

She shook her head. "I don't know. It was turned over. Maybe the person's I'm talking to."

"Maybe. Any idea who that might be? Man or woman, even?"

She shook her head. "This is going to sound weird but it makes me sad to think of that person. I don't even know who it is. How can I be sad?"

"You know the person. You just can't remember him or her right now. But there's emotion connected to that knowing. Are you sure it's sadness? Could you be mad? Disappointed?"

"Sad. And maybe angry. Those don't seem to go together."

"Tell me about the laptop?"

She closed her eyes. "A big one. Maybe a seventeen-inch screen."

"What was on the screen?"

"I don't know. Information. I don't know what. I was pointing at something. Telling somebody to go online for the mileage form."

They were both quiet for several more miles. She turned to him. "What do you think it means?"

"It means that things are coming back. It's only a matter of time."

"It's hard to be patient when I feel so anxious. When I feel that I'm fighting time."

STORMY WAS PROBABLY right to feel as if she was fighting time. With every hour that went by, the Mercedes Men had more of an opportunity to track him to Ravesville. He wondered if he should move Stormy now. Take her a couple thousand miles away, where he didn't have to worry about pulling into a damn gas station and the potential of somebody seeing her.

The idea was certainly attractive. But he suspected maybe counterproductive. Her memory was coming back. And it was impossible to know what sight or sound might break the logjam in her head. But he was fairly confident that the stimuli weren't a thousand miles away.

What he was more confident of was her reaction if he mentioned getting away from it all. She'd refuse. She dealt with things head-on. From that first night in the hotel, when she'd casually walked past him with shampoo in her hands, ready to disable him the first chance she got, she'd shown her considerable backbone.

She'd hung on to the side of a damn truck, in the middle of the snowstorm, no coat, no shoes, probably still partially drugged up. She was a fighter.

And he'd yet to hear her whine or complain about *why me?* Sure, she'd expressed frustration over her inability to remember but there'd been no prolonged pity parties. She was handling this about as well as anybody might hope.

By the time he pulled into his driveway, the sun had set. Still, with a full moon, it was a light night. Everything looked the same. No fresh tracks in the snow from someone else approaching the house. He backed into the garage and they got out. Just to be sure, he carried the groceries in one hand and his gun in the other.

They were shutting the front door behind them when he heard the sound of an approaching vehicle.

Chapter Thirteen

"Go," he told her. "Upstairs. Not your room. Use the first bedroom. It has a deeper closet. Get all the way in the back. Don't come out, no matter what you hear."

There was no time to argue. The engine was closer. The vehicle was turning into the driveway.

She was halfway up the stairs before she made the decision that she wasn't going to let him fight the battle alone. He was in danger because of her. She glanced over her shoulder and he was watching her, making sure she got to safety before he opened the door.

She wasn't going to screw with his concentration but she also wasn't going to hide like some scared third grader. She opened the first door. It smelled of fresh paint. She closed it behind her just as she heard a car door slam.

She glanced at the windows across the room. They did her no good. They faced the backyard, giving her no view of the driveway and who might have come to the house.

She waited for a second slam, thinking that was the pattern of the Mercedes Men. Two approached. Two waited behind in backup. But there was only one car door.

She heard a knock at the front door, then the quiet rustle of Cal moving toward it. Just as he opened the front door, she quietly opened the bedroom door and slipped down the hall.

Hidden crouched behind the half wall, she now could hear everything that was being said. Of course, if they came up the stairs, she was a sitting duck. There was no place to run.

"Hi," she heard a feminine voice say. "I...uh...was looking for Chase."

"He's not here," Cal said. His voice was polite, but not friendly.

"Where is he?" she asked. Her tone had a little more edge.

There was a pause. "Who wants to know?" Cal asked.

She risked a look around the edge of the wall. From her angle, she could see the woman who still stood in the doorway. She was beautiful. Tall. Slender. And she had the most amazing red hair. It flowed to her waist. She was staring intently at Cal.

"Oh my gosh," the woman said. "You're Calvin, aren't you? I haven't seen you for almost ten years."

"Trish?" he said, his voice warmer. "Trish Wright?"

"Wright-Roper," she said. "What are you doing here?"

Cal stepped back, enough that Trish could step into the house and close the door behind her. The flow of cold air that had been making its way up the stairs was cut off.

She had no idea who Trish Wright-Roper was but clearly, Cal didn't think this woman was a threat. She started to breathe a little easier.

"Just got out of the navy," he said. "Came home for Thanksgiving. How's your sister?" he asked.

"Summer is good. Divorced recently. But she's got two great kids that I spoil rotten."

"And you're married?" he said.

"Widowed," she replied softly. "Listen, I don't want you to think I'm crazy since we're just reconnecting after a really long time but Summer and I own the Wright Here, Wright Now Café in Ravesville. Just a little while ago, some men came in, asking for directions to the Hollister house."

That wasn't good.

"There was something about them. Summer and I both had the same feel. They said they were looking for their cousin and asked if we'd seen a dark-haired woman. Now, that certainly didn't sound like Raney but still, it was an odd exchange. We've gotten to know Raney and wouldn't want anything to happen to her. So when I gave them the directions, I gave them good ones, but the long way around. The minute they left, I tried the house phone but there was no answer. I realized I didn't know Chase's cell phone. I jumped in the car and came here to warn him. You've probably only got about fifteen minutes before they show up."

"How many men?" Cal asked, his voice even.

"Two. I saw two."

"Okay," Cal said. "Thank you. This is very helpful. But you need to get out of here."

"Do you want me to go to the police? Of course, my ex-brother-in-law is probably on duty and he's not likely to be helpful."

"Nope. I've got this," Cal said. "But you're right. These men aren't friends of the Hollister family. But you and Summer need to be careful around them. Don't give them any reason to believe that you'd side with us."

She heard the door open, felt the cold air whoosh in.

"Be careful, Cal. Men like you, men like my Rafe, you think you can handle anything but sometimes it's just too much." Her voice was full of emotion.

"Don't worry," Cal assured her. "I got this covered. I'll be in for breakfast soon. Be careful driving in the dark."

"Good to see you again, Cal," the woman said, her voice fading away.

"You, too, Trish. And thanks again." Cal shut the door.

She was debating how best to get back to the closet when she heard Cal's boot on the first step.

"You can come out from behind the wall now," he said.

She stood up. He didn't look mad, more resigned.

"How did you know I was there?"

"Really excellent hearing," he said. "I heard the click of the door, saw just a shadow of movement as I was opening the front door and realized what you were doing. I had some level of confidence that you'd figure out a way to stay hidden," he added.

"I did," she said somewhat unnecessarily.

He nodded. "So you heard everything?"

"Yes. Who is she?"

"Trish Wright. I guess, Wright-Roper now. My brother Bray dated her sister Summer for years. We all thought they'd end up married but it didn't happen that way. Bray went away to the marines and Summer married somebody else. I appreciate the fact that they've still got kind feelings toward the Hollister family." Cal looked at his watch. "We've got less than ten minutes. This time, I really do need you to hide. Will you do that? Please?"

"Tell me your plan first," she said, not answering his question.

"I don't have one," he said. "Other than to get more information out of them than they get from me and to keep you safe. Everything besides that is fluid."

She let out a loud breath.

"I can't focus on them if in the back of my mind I'm wondering what you're doing," he said.

"Fine," she said. "I'll be in the back of the closet, hidden behind the clothes." She started to walk toward the bedroom.

"Stormy," he said.

She stopped. "Yes."

He put his hand on her shoulder, turned her and kissed her. All the emotion of the moment was packed into ten seconds of scorching pleasure.

Then he stepped back. "We're not finished," he said.

CAL WAS ON the porch, swinging in the old hammock, whittling on a stick when the Mercedes Men drove into the yard. He turned the outside porch light on, making it easy for them to see him. He wore an old military jacket that he'd gotten soon after he'd enlisted. After Stormy had gone upstairs, he'd quickly pulled it from his duffel bag. It had seen better days but he'd always been reluctant to part with it.

One car drove in. Two men inside. He figured the second car was probably just over the hill.

Both men opened their car doors. They appeared to be unarmed but Cal figured they had plenty of fire-power on them and in the car.

"Hello," the driver said. He was the man who had done the talking in the hotel. Cal was confident that this was G. On the passenger side was the guy who walked funny, the one he'd coined Bad Knee.

"Hello," Cal said easily. He kept whittling. Small pieces of wood littered the snow-covered porch.

"Kind of cold to be outside," G said.

"I'm watching for 'em," Cal said.

The two men looked at each other. "For who?" Bad Knee asked.

Cal looked up, his eyes darting fast. "The jerks in the woods. I'll blow this place up before I'll let them take it." He held up his knife. "I'm ready."

"You were in the military," G said, focusing on his jacket.

Cal nodded. "Just got home. Had to drive through a storm to get here. I told everybody I saw along the way that they were coming."

The two men exchanged another glance. He wasn't sure if they remembered him from seeing him by the vending machines. They had barely given him a glance that night. But now, Cal was pretty confident that they thought he was relatively harmless. "Our car is having trouble," G explained. "We barely got it here. May we use your phone to call for help?"

"I guess," Cal said, getting up. "You two from around here?"

"Nope. Just passing through," said Bad Knee.

Cal showed them the phone in the kitchen. As they walked through the house, they looked in every room. Bad Knee was eyeing the upstairs.

"Big house for a single guy," Bad Knee said.

"My brother lives here, too," Cal said. "Cried like a little girl about the snowstorm. We had to stop driving and spent the night at a hotel." He was pretty confident the hotel clerk might have told these two about the man and his brother who had stayed in room 14. "He went to get beer."

"I see," said Bad Knee. "We're in the area looking for our cousin. She ran away from home."

"I did that once," Cal said, grinning big.

"It's not a good thing," G said. "She's young. Foolish. Has dark hair. She's very beautiful," he added somewhat bitterly.

"She better be careful. They can see in the dark. Like a damn cat," he said. He took his knife and drew a line down the dark woodwork, marring it. "Ticktock, goes the clock." He tapped his knife against the woodwork.

The two men walked toward the door.

"You can stay here and wait for a ride if you want," Cal said.

"No. That's okay. We'll be going," G said.

"You got any matches?" Cal asked.

The driver frowned. "Matches? Why?"

"I got to start a fire. They don't like fire."

G chuckled. "Sure. I got some matches." He pulled a half-used matchbook from his pocket. "Make it a good one," he added, flipping it toward Cal.

The men walked back to their car, got in and drove off. Cal sat back down on the hammock and continued his whittling. He didn't move for three minutes. When he was sure the cars had moved on, he got up, walked inside and locked the door behind him. He took off his coat and tossed it on the couch in the living room.

Unfinished business. That was what he had with Stormy.

Halfway up the stairs, he called out her name. "Stormy."

She didn't answer. He walked into the room, strode over to the closet and ripped the clothes out of the way. Held out a hand and hauled her out of the small space. Once she was out, in one smooth movement, she wrapped her arms around his neck, her legs around his waist, and kissed him for all he was worth.

He could have kissed her all day. But all too soon, she unwrapped her legs and slid down his body. He was painfully aroused and he doubted that she wasn't fully aware of the fact.

"I was scared," she admitted, her hand resting on his chest. "I thought you might kill them."

"I would have," he said, "if it had been necessary. But the other two would have come looking for them eventually and then I'd have had to kill them, too. Even though I really wanted to beat the crap out of them for what they did to you, it just didn't seem like the most prudent action to take right now. They're a clue to your identity. The more we ultimately learn about them, perhaps the more we learn about you."

"I appreciate your restraint," she said, sounding half serious, half amused.

Restraint was not ripping her clothes off and taking her with her back against the wall. He shrugged. "Maybe they'll give up."

She shook her head. "You don't really think that, do you?"

"No. I bought us a little space. They'll be back or we'll run into them somewhere along the way."

"But they won't be back right away." Her tone was suggestive and he could feel hope rise in his chest. But this was too important to have any potential misread of the situation.

"I want to make sure I'm clear here," he said, his damn voice cracking. "I want to take you to bed, Stormy. And if you don't want that, we need to stop. Now."

She moved the hand that had rested on his chest to the back of his neck. She pulled his head down, met him halfway, her lips still wet from the earlier kisses. When she stuck her tongue into his mouth, he felt the answering surge in his body. When the kiss ended, she pulled back just a little. "Don't stop. Please don't stop."

"Just so you know, we're about one minute shy of doing this on the floor versus on a soft mattress."

She threw her head back and laughed. Then she jumped and wrapped her legs around his waist one more time.

HE CARRIED HER into his old room, gently dumped her down onto the mattress and fell in beside her. And it took almost no time for them to be naked. And for him to be inside her.

It was…amazing. He had his hands under her rear and his strokes were long and purposeful and she was just this close to—

She came explosively, her internal muscles clamping down.

"That's my girl," he murmured in her ear.

And when she was finally spent, he spread her even wider and went deeper. Minutes later, he tightened, groaned and emptied into her.

Or rather the condom. He had had the good sense to have one in his pocket.

"That's my boy," she said, slightly modifying his comment. She patted his back, which was damp with sweat.

He smiled against her shoulder. He was careful to keep his weight off her. After a minute, he said, "That was pretty fast. You okay?"

"Wonderful. Thanks…uh…for having protection."

He shifted, withdrew and rolled to his side. He pulled on her hip, turning her, so that they were facing. "I need you to understand something," he said. "I'm a young, single guy. So I keep some condoms in my bag. But I need you to know, I don't…" He stopped and shook his head. "I don't go through that many," he finished.

She wanted to laugh but he was so serious. "I get that, Cal. You're not promiscuous. I…I don't think I am, either."

In fact, it felt as if she'd used some muscles that didn't get used all that much. But it had been worth it. And while it had been fast, it hadn't been too fast.

Truth be told, she'd have let him take her on the floor.

Now she couldn't wait to share with him what had happened while she was in the closet. "I remembered something," she said.

HIS HEAD SNAPPED UP.

"It was hearing the voices. The one who said that it was a big house for one person."

"That's the guy with the bad knee."

"Yeah. That makes sense. Remember that I told you about the ghost. And that I was afraid of him. It was him. He's the ghost."

Cal propped himself up on one elbow. "How do you know?"

"He's the one who drugged me. Shots in the arm. After I saw the wedding dress in the corner of the room, he gave me a shot. When I woke up, I was wearing the dress and my head hurt. I didn't realize it was a veil until they let me up. I tried to pull it off and he slapped me."

"I should have killed him," Cal said.

She patted his arm. "That's my boy," she said, repeating what she'd said earlier.

He managed a grudging smile.

"Anyway, then he dragged me down some hallway. I tried to resist but they'd put these stupid shoes on me and I couldn't get any traction. But I saw the way he walked. The way he swung his leg from the hip. I think…" She stopped, closing her eyes. "I thought he was a ghost but he was just a stupid man wearing a sheet that he'd cut eye and mouth holes into. He never wanted me to see his face."

There was only one reason for that. They hadn't intended to kill her. Drug her, yes. Keep her captive, sure. But they weren't going to kill her because one of them intended to marry her.

It was a crazy plan. And didn't seem well thought out. What did they think she was going to do once they got complacent and stopped drugging her? Be happy that she'd been forced into a marriage?

No. That wouldn't happen. They would know that she would run the first opportunity she got.

Unless there was no place to run.

Where had they intended to take her? Why?

There were so many questions. But it was good to finally have some solid proof that there hadn't been any plan to kill her. Maybe that would work in her favor if they found her.

Not that he intended to let that happen.

But bullets killed and something could happen to him. "Listen," he said, "I'm going to get you my brothers' phone numbers. You need to memorize them. If something happens to me, go to them. Brayden Hollister. Like I said before, he's DEA and one tough son of a gun. He's in New York. And Chase Hollister. Detective with the St. Louis Police Department."

She put her hand on his arm. "Don't worry," she said. "We're both going to be okay."

She's very beautiful. That was what G had said. It was the same thing he'd said to the hotel clerk. In his gut, Cal knew that this was the man who had not only purchased the wedding dress but had also been the one who intended to marry Stormy. When he'd described Stormy, there had been deep emotion. Not love. Obsession, perhaps. Tinged now with a heavy dose of anger.

A dangerous combination.

"Maybe it's time to go to the police," he said. "Your memory is coming back. You've got enough to tell them."

She shook her head. "I can't trust the police."

"Why?"

"I don't know. But in my heart, I know that to be true."

He could call Chase. Maybe Chase could put some feelers out, see if there was any information within the law enforcement world circulating about Stormy.

But Chase had his hands full. Someone he loved was testifying at a murder trial. Cal wasn't going to ask him to put his own interests second again in favor of Cal's interest. He just wouldn't.

The Mercedes Men surely wouldn't be back for at least another couple days. He'd give Stormy another forty-eight hours and then they had to do something.

"I should get up," she said. "It's close to eight. You've got to be hungry."

"You bet," he said, leaning down and nuzzling her pretty breast.

Chapter Fourteen

Cal was very talented with his mouth. No debating that, she thought, as she cracked eggs in a bowl. She was making French toast for a very late dinner.

It had been an amazing day. It seemed only fitting that the day had culminated with several hours in Cal's bed.

She was slightly sore and deliciously satisfied. It was a nice combination.

"Hey," he said, coming up behind her. He was freshly showered and he smelled of soap and mint from the toothpaste he'd used. He wrapped an arm around her waist and turned her to face him. Then he kissed her.

"Your French toast will burn," she said, pulling back.

"I don't care," he said.

She gave him a gentle push. "I think we need to go back and see Pietro. He wasn't happy that I knocked on his door. That must mean something."

"It's probably worth a try."

She flipped three pieces of French toast onto a plate. She handed it to him.

"Thank you," he said. He waited until she'd gotten her own serving and sat down at the table before he cut into his food. "Good," he said between bites.

She could probably feed him dog food and he'd be appreciative. She took a bite and chewed slowly.

"I need to ask you something," she said.

"Okay."

"Don't ask me to hide in the closet again," she said. "I don't think I can do it. I need to be able to help."

He looked her in the eye. "I understand. I do. But I'm not going to let you get hurt. I can't."

"I feel the same toward you," she said.

He seemed to consider that. Something changed in his eyes. She saw a bleak look of what might have been disgust.

"I'm sorry," he said. "I made a mistake."

She'd wanted him to understand, not to be defeated. "I understand, I do. It's just—"

"I need to tell you something."

Something in the tone of his voice told her that this was her opportunity to be strong for him. "I'm listening," she said.

"I told you that my stepfather wasn't a nice guy. That was an understatement. He was a mean bastard."

She kept her mouth shut. She'd sort of figured that.

"I haven't always looked like this," he said.

That made her smile. "You weren't born 6'2" and 200 pounds?"

He shook his head. But he seemed to have relaxed just a little. "I didn't hit my growth spurt until college. I was thin as a rail in middle school and high school."

She wasn't sure where this was going.

"Chase was three years older and a foot taller and seventy pounds heavier. But he was still no match for Brick."

Things were becoming clearer.

"Brick used to beat him," Cal said. "Sometimes badly."

Her heart broke for the young boy he'd been. He'd had to have seen that. Probably had to worry that he was next.

"He didn't hit me."

"That was good. Right?" she asked.

"You know why? You want to know why?" his voice rose.

She wasn't sure she did but she figured he was going to tell her. "Why?" she asked softly.

"Because Chase made a bargain with him. Brick could beat on him all he wanted. Chase wouldn't fight back and he wouldn't turn him in. In exchange, Brick was to keep his hands off me."

Oh my. "I think your brother must have loved you very much," she said finally.

He ignored the comment. "You know how I found out? Brick told me. He and my mother came to my college graduation. The college that Chase had paid for, sometimes working three jobs at a time. And that was my present from Brick Doogan. He told me the truth."

"Why?"

"Because I think he knew that it would tear Chase and me apart. And that made him happy."

"Did it? Tear you apart?"

"I was so angry with Chase. So angry with myself that I hadn't been smarter, that I hadn't seen what was happening. That I'd ignored the clues that I'd seen. Because I was afraid."

"You were a child."

Cal didn't say anything for a long minute. "When I

asked you to hide in the closet, I was doing the same thing that Chase had done for me. Protecting. For good reason, perhaps. But it was the wrong thing to do."

"I'm not angry," she said.

"I was. After Brick told me, I couldn't keep my head on straight. The underlying message was clear. *You can't protect yourself so I'll do it for you. No matter what the cost to me.*" How the hell was something like that supposed to make a guy feel?

Emasculated. Impotent. "What did you say to Chase?"

"Nothing. I couldn't. As fast as I could, I enlisted in the navy and left home. Chase was shocked, to say the least. I'd just graduated with a mechanical engineering degree. I'd never talked about enlisting. And suddenly, I was in and on my way to basic training."

"Why did you do it?"

"I had to. I had something to prove. That I didn't need anybody fighting my battles. I was determined to be the best, the toughest. Nobody would ever have to take care of me again. When an opportunity came up to become a SEAL, I didn't hesitate."

She sat quietly, processing everything that he'd said. "And you and Chase have never talked about this."

"Nope. I sort of stopped talking to him at all. Look, I'm not proud of that but I was twenty-two and very angry with him. Yet, I loved him and knew that I owed him a great deal. With those conflicting emotions, I felt it was better to just be away. Chase and I have communicated over the years but we've never really talked. That's why I was coming home this Thanksgiving. It's time. Past time."

She understood much better that myriad of emotions she heard in his voice whenever he talked about his brother. "I'm betting that's going to be a really good conversation," she said. "You'll handle it beautifully."

He shrugged. "We'll see. He needs to understand that I'm not angry any longer. I get why he did what he did." He looked her in the eye. "And I will try very hard to never ask you to hide in another closet."

"Thank you," she said softly. "And thank you for telling me about Brick and about Chase. You know, you've got your head on pretty straight."

He shrugged. "I thought you should know, especially since we…"

"We did it," she teased, wanting desperately to lighten the mood.

"Yeah. Since we did it." He stood up and stretched, yawning widely. "I'm still real happy about that, you know."

She felt warm. "I'm probably going to turn in shortly," she said. "I'm hoping that you're not planning on sleeping downstairs." She wanted him in her bed. She wanted his heat, his strength, his incredible maleness to surround her. To insulate her from the rest of the world.

She wanted him inside her again.

She held out her hand. "Come with me."

WHEN SHE WOKE UP the next morning, Cal was already awake. He was watching her. "Hi," she said, a little self-conscious. "What are you looking at?"

He smiled. "Dessert."

She raised an eyebrow. "As I recall, you had a couple *helpings* last night."

"There are certain times when it's just damn foolish to count calories."

She'd been counting orgasms. Four.

"Remember anything else while you were sleeping?" he asked, his tone gentle.

She shook her head. "Today will be the day. I just know it."

"I know you have your hopes pinned on what we might get from Pietro but I don't want you to be disappointed."

She sat up in bed. When the sheet dropped to her waist, she pulled it up fast but not before Cal gave her a look of pure male appreciation. "Of course I'll be disappointed. But not devastated. There's a difference." She smoothed down the sheet, running the palm of her hand over it several times. "It's Friday. I think I'm running out of time."

He nodded. "So we should get up and get going."

She would much rather stay in bed and play. "Yes," she said, already swinging her legs over the side.

They ate a quick breakfast of cereal and toast. When they walked outside, she could tell the weather had warmed up considerably, probably to the midforties. That, combined with the sunny day, was making the remaining snow and ice melt quickly.

When they passed Fitzler's, she didn't tease him any more about buying the property. But she saw him take a long look, as if he might be sizing the place up.

When they got to the spot where Cal had found her, there were spots in the vast expanse of land where the ground, an ugly green-brown, showed through. It looked so different than it had just forty-eight hours before.

But then again, she was very different, too.

A woman couldn't leave Cal Hollister's bed unchanged.

Cal had touched her heart, too. Of course she was different. When he'd listened and really *heard* her request to not be shuffled to the back of the closet, she'd known that something powerful had happened. It had been a connection that she still wasn't sure she understood but it had told her everything she needed to know about Cal Hollister and the kind of man he was.

They pulled into the diner parking lot and went through the same routine as before. She got out of sight, Cal checked the parking lot, then entered the diner alone. At three minutes, she followed.

Unfortunately, Lena wasn't working. It was a younger waitress who was hurrying back and forth with coffee and heaping plates of food.

She slid into the booth, anxious to see if there was any sign of recognition. It was impossible to know how many people G had shown her picture to. "Coffee?" the waitress asked, barely giving them a glance. Her name tag said Laura.

They both nodded and Laura hurried away, presumably to get them cups. Cal got up from the booth and snagged a newspaper off the stack that was haphazardly lying at the end of the counter. He sat back down and started quickly scanning the contents, flipping through the pages.

"Looking for something in particular?" she asked.

"Nope. Just looking," he said.

She didn't believe that. Cal probably never did anything without intention.

He pushed the newspaper in her direction. "Why don't you take a look?"

She shrugged. "Can't hurt," she said. The front page

was primarily devoted to national news and then it turned more local on the inside pages. She scanned the obituaries and passed up the food ads. The second section of the paper was Sports.

And the hair on the back of her neck stood up. Her hand hovered over the page, anxious to flip, not able to complete the action.

"What?" Cal asked immediately.

Laura chose that moment to return to the table, two coffee cups in one hand, setting them down with a thud.

She watched as Laura took a pen out of her pocket. At least somebody was acting in a normal, expected manner. Not like her, who practically had a panic attack over a newspaper. What the hell was wrong with her?

"What can I get you this morning?" Laura asked.

Instead of ordering, Cal looked toward the kitchen. "We were hoping to catch up with Pietro while we were here," he said.

"Good luck," Laura said. "He didn't show this morning."

Her hand started to shake. She put down her coffee cup before the liquid sloshed over the rim. "Is he sick?"

Laura shrugged and looked toward the door as a table of four came in. "Not sure. But he hasn't called in and the owner is really pissed. He's acting like Pietro does this all the time. I've worked here for over a year and have never seen it before. The guy is a jerk."

"Pietro?" Cal attempted to clarify.

"No. The owner." She tapped her pen on the order pad. "What would you like?"

Cal pushed the menus to the edge of the table. "We'll take four of your cinnamon rolls to go and if you could put these coffees in some paper cups, that would be great." He pulled a twenty out of his shirt pocket. "You can keep the change."

Laura scooped up the money and their coffee cups. "I'll be right back."

"What do you think?" she asked once the woman was out of hearing range.

"It's odd," Cal admitted. "And when odd things happen, we should pay attention. But first, tell me about the newspaper."

"There's something here," she said, her voice soft. "I can feel it."

"Which article?"

She looked at the Sports section again. There was a big article about the St. Louis Blues hockey team, a smaller article about coaching changes in the National Baseball League and several blurbs about local sporting events coming up on the weekend.

"None of them," she admitted. "It's just an overall sense of unease."

"You have a lot of sports knowledge," he said. "For a girl," he added, his tone teasing.

As always, Cal had the most amazing way of adding just a little humor right when it was desperately needed. "We need to find Pietro."

"Agreed. That's why we're taking our stuff to go."

In less than three minutes, they were in the car. Once they got out of the parking lot and back onto the highway, Cal drove with one hand and held a cinnamon roll in the other. She felt too nervous to eat but she sipped her coffee.

"How do we play this?" she asked as they got closer.

"I've been thinking about that." He took a big drink of coffee. "I think we need to be prepared for the possibility that something happened to him. After all, to unexpectedly not show for work and not call..."

Her coffee started to roll in her stomach. "You think something happened to him because he talked to me?"

"I don't know. But it does seem odd that your conversation was yesterday and today, this."

"I'm like the damn plague," she said, so irritated with the whole situation that she could barely stand it. She wanted to thump her head against the window, to shake loose the memories that refused to come back.

"You might be the catalyst but you're not the person responsible for anything that's happening," he said. "And I could be way off. I said we simply needed to be prepared."

He wasn't wrong. Something had happened to Pietro and it likely had something to do with her and the Mercedes Men.

When they got close to Pietro's house, Cal did a pass-by, the same as the day before. Nothing appeared different. The snow had melted enough that the car tracks from the day before were no longer visible. Now there were simply patches of snow, split by long strips of gravel.

She expected Cal to stop like before, so that he could get out and she could drive. Instead, he did a U-turn and headed back toward Pietro's. "We're going in together?" she said.

"Yeah. I would prefer to leave you alongside the road while I go check but I figured you wouldn't be too happy about that."

He had remembered that she'd asked him not to leave her out, to include her in her own defense.

"Thank you," she said.

"Don't thank me yet," he said, his tone disgusted. "This could be the stupidest thing I've ever done. We need to be prepared for the possibility that the Mercedes Men found out about your visit and that they are betting that you'll come back. They may be waiting for us."

"Then we deal with them," she said. "We need to stop this before more people get involved."

He didn't respond. When he made the turn into Pietro's driveway, he glanced at her. "Be ready," he said.

"I am." She sincerely hoped that they did not find Pietro dead in his house. She wasn't sure how she felt about a potential confrontation with the Mercedes Men. She'd been truthful when she'd said she wanted this over with. But she certainly didn't want to put Cal in danger.

"I go first," he said. "Stay behind me."

"Okay. What if he's inside, on the couch, with the flu? What are we going to tell him?"

"We'll have to think of something."

Nobody shot at them as they walked from the SUV to the front door. Cal knocked sharply. She listened carefully for any telltale noise from inside and knew Cal was doing the same.

But they heard nothing.

Cal tried the door. It was locked.

He hesitated for just seconds before removing the tool from his pocket and picking the lock. Then he wrapped his hand in his shirttail before turning the knob.

The interior was dark. Quiet. They went into the kitchen, which looked out into the backyard, similar to the Hollister house. But the similarities ended there. While the Hollister appliances were thirty years old, these were brand-new stainless steel. There was a six-burner stove with double ovens. Big pans with copper bottoms hung from hooks in the ceiling.

All of that was interesting but not as interesting as the plate on the counter. It was a sandwich, with four or five bites out of it. There was a half a slice of fresh pineapple.

It appeared that Pietro's lunch had been interrupted.

"I'm going to look in the bedrooms," Cal whispered.

She nodded. The kitchen smelled like…cinnamon. Yes, that was it. She opened the oven. Inside was the remains of some kind of crumble. It looked half-baked.

Pietro had had the presence of mind to shut off his oven but he hadn't wanted to waste any time waiting for the dessert to finish cooking.

Cal came back into the kitchen. "The house is empty. No signs of struggle. I'm going to check the garage."

His car wasn't going to be there. She was confident of that. When Cal came back in just a minute, he shook his head. "He's gone," he said.

"He was in a hurry."

"Looks like it," Cal agreed. "There's no way of knowing what he took for clothes or where he might be headed. Let's get out of here."

"Wait," she said. She walked over to the desk in the corner of the kitchen. She used a pen to pick through the mail, flipping envelopes over.

"What are you looking for?" he asked.

"Two things. His last name. There's an electric bill here for Pietro Moroque. And—" she stopped and smiled at him "—this." She pointed to a bright orange envelope. Like Cal had with the door, she used her shirt-tail to pull out the card from inside. It was a Halloween card. A child had scribbled his name inside. It was hard to read but she thought it said Jacob. She didn't care about that. She looked at the envelope. The return address in the corner was a preprinted address sticker. *Tika Moroque. 519 Feather Ave., Kansas City, MO 64110.*

"This has got to be his wife and child," she said. "If he's running, will he go there first to say goodbye?"

"Or to make sure they're safe?" Cal said.

With her shirt, she carefully wiped off the pen that she'd touched. She tossed it back onto the desk. "Let's go."

Chapter Fifteen

It took a couple hours to reach Kansas City but they had no trouble finding Tika Moroque's house. Their GPS led them right to it. It was a modest ranch on a quiet street. There was a swing set in the backyard with a big slide.

They made a pass-by in both directions before parking on the street, across from the house. They got out, crossed the street, walked up the short sidewalk and rang the bell.

It was almost noon on a Friday and there was no reason to believe that anyone would be home. Still, they waited. And rang the doorbell a second time.

Just as they were about to return to the car, the front door swung open. A woman, dark short hair, maybe midthirties, wearing a gray business suit, answered the door.

Before Cal or she could speak, the woman held up her index finger and pointed at them. "You need to get the hell away from my house."

"We just want a minute of your time, ma'am," Cal said.

"No, you don't," she said. "You want to screw up my life. And the life I've built for my son. But I'm not going to let you. Get off my porch." She tried to close the door but Cal was faster.

He stuck his foot in the door and pushed forward. In just seconds, they were inside the small house.

The woman had her back against the wall with her hand up to her mouth. She looked scared to death.

Now it was Cal's turn to hold up a finger. "We are not going to hurt you. Or your son. Let me be clear about that. But I didn't want to have this conversation on the street."

"I have nothing to say to you," she said.

"Well, we have something to tell you." Cal motioned to the small living room at his right. "Perhaps we could sit?"

Tika finally nodded. She took small sideways steps, never taking her eyes off them. When they sat on the couch, she lowered herself into the chair opposite of them.

"My name is Cal Hollister. This is Stormy. I call her Stormy because I found her three days ago, injured and alone, in the middle of a snowstorm."

They had the woman's attention. Her eyes were big.

"Unfortunately," Cal continued, "Stormy doesn't remember her real name or how she ended up in the snowstorm. She had a head injury."

Tika didn't say anything but her face looked less frightened.

"We went to see your ex-husband yesterday. We had reason to believe that he might be able to help us. But he wasn't helpful. And today, when we tried to talk to him again, he's suddenly gone from his house and missing from work."

Tika showed no reaction to the news. They weren't surprising her.

"We need your help. That's all we want." Cal sat back on the couch.

She felt like squirming under Tika's stare. But she sat still, with her hands calmly folded in her lap.

"You really can't remember who you are?" Tika finally asked.

She shook her head. "I'm hoping you can help me with that."

"I have no idea," Tika said.

She tried not to let the disappointment swamp her. She needed to think. "But our visit here didn't surprise you," she said.

Tika shook her head. "My ex-husband was waiting for me as I left the day care this morning after dropping off my son. I was on my way to work but after we talked, I decided to come home. I wasn't up to facing the office. He told me about your visit to his house yesterday."

"What did he tell you?"

Tika hesitated. Then she shrugged. "He said that he'd catered a wedding reception for an old acquaintance from Moldaire College. That he hadn't wanted to but he owed the man and this would pay the debt."

"Owed?" Cal asked.

Tika shook her head. "I don't know the details. I don't want to know. There were things about my ex-husband that I discovered after we were married that didn't make me happy. That's one of the reasons we're no longer married."

"He said the man had showed him a picture of his fiancée and when you came to his door, he knew that you were the same woman. He also knew that something had gone wrong. The man had come with some friends to pick up the food. They made one trip out to their car but there was more stuff. He was waiting for them to come back for the second load. They didn't. Finally, he went outside to see what was going on. They were very agitated. They didn't realize that Pietro speaks Russian. They were talking about how the woman had disappeared. About that time a couple cops drove in and the men got the hell out of there, without ever getting the rest of the food."

"Pietro asked me about the roast pork and rosemary potatoes."

"Yeah," Tika said. "That's what they left behind. When you said it was good, he knew you were lying."

"Can you tell me the names of the men?" Cal asked.

She shook her head. "I don't know their names. I don't want to know their names. He referred to the man who had contacted him as Golya. I don't know if that's a first or last name."

Cal showed no reaction to the name. She understood. There was no reason for Tika to know that it meant something to them. "Did he contact Golya and tell him that we'd been at his house?" she asked.

Tika shook her head. "No. That's why he decided he needed to disappear for a few days. He said that if Golya found out that the missing woman had been at his house and that he'd simply let her go, he would be very angry. Maybe angry enough to kill him."

"Why did he let me go?"

"I got the impression that he thinks Golya is crazy. Like really crazy as in mentally ill. He did say the man is a mean son of a bitch and he didn't want any part of sending you back to him. I really do think my ex is trying to be a better person."

"How would Golya have found out Stormy was there?" Cal asked.

Tika pointed her finger in their general direction. "Even without his help, Pietro was confident Golya would find her. And then he assumed that she would probably tell Golya about the visit, not realizing the jeopardy it would put Pietro in. Unfortunately, he didn't think about this until he'd let her drive away."

"So he was simply going to hide forever?" Cal asked, shaking his head.

"Not forever. He seemed to think that Golya was headed back to Russia very soon, maybe within days."

"Why did he think that?" she asked.

"Something Golya said about his bride learning to love Russia when it was her new home."

She looked at Cal. If she hadn't managed to get away, would they have somehow managed to get her out of the United States and into Russia?

"We really need to know more about Golya," Cal said. "Surely you can contact your ex-husband. He would have given you some way to do that in the event something happened to your son."

Tika shook her head. "There was no need. I have sole custody of my son. I am his mother. Pietro is not his father. Another reason why our marriage didn't work. My son does not understand the particulars yet. He is too small. The truth is known by just a few people. But if something happens to my son, I would call his real father, not Pietro."

"Given that, it seems odd to me that he came here this morning," she said. "Why tell you all this?"

Tika shrugged. "I don't think he has anybody else. And to tell you the truth, I think he just wanted somebody to know in case he did suddenly turn up dead. I wish he wouldn't have. I'd rather not know." Tika stood up and looked at her watch. "When I saw the two of you on the porch, I wasn't going to answer the door. I don't want any of this ugliness touching me. But then I figured that you'd probably just come back and Jacob might be here then."

Tika walked over and opened the front door. "I've told you everything I know. Now I'm asking you nicely. Please just leave my house and forget that we ever had this conversation because that's what I'm going to do."

She stood up. "I know you said that you couldn't get a message to Pietro. But if you could," she added, "you can assure him that I won't say anything about seeing him to the men who hired him to do the catering. It's not my intent to put anyone else in danger."

Tika shrugged. "I got the impression from Pietro that these are not nice people. You should probably be worried about yourself."

She and Cal were back in the car before Cal spoke again. "It's starting to make some sense," he said.

"How's that?" she asked, shaking her head.

"Most of the time, kidnappers never intend to return the victim. They keep the person until they are no longer valuable to them and then dispose of them. For that reason, they rarely care if their victim can describe them. But in your case, it was different. The person who interacted with you, the Ghost, was careful that you couldn't identify him."

"He never hurt me. Just kept me drugged up and then

got me dressed in that awful wedding dress. I don't understand why G would think that I would be any happier being his bride in Russia than in the United States."

"Tika said that Pietro thought he was mentally ill. Maybe he was confident that he could win you over. Maybe he thought you'd fall in love with Russia. Maybe he was going to keep putting pills in your coffee so that you were a little doped up for the next twenty years."

"But why?"

"That's easy," Cal said. "You're very beautiful. To a man like him, having you as his wife would be a great accomplishment."

She looked at her still-bruised wrists. "He would have had to tie me to the bed for the next twenty years."

"There are other forms of coercion that make a person stay in a bad marriage," he said, his tone gentle.

She didn't need him to spell it out. What would have happened if she'd gotten pregnant? Even if she despised the father, she would never have left her child behind.

"We need to go to Moldaire. I know it's dangerous but time is running out."

"If indeed there is something significant about Saturday," he countered.

"There is," she said. "I know it."

He put the car in gear. "We can be there in forty-five minutes. We may want to make a stop on the way."

"Where?"

"When G and Bad Knee were at the house, I could smell cigar smoke on them. I asked if they had any matches. They tossed me a half-used book. It was from someplace called Raftors. I did a quick search this morning. It's a lingerie shop."

"Lingerie? Is that code for something?"

He shook his head. "Appears legit. At least the front of the house. Not sure what goes on in the back rooms."

"Why didn't you say anything before this?" she asked.

"I thought you might get a little freaked out thinking about G buying lingerie."

"It makes me sick," she admitted. "Because it was probably going to be presented to me on my wedding night. But it's a clue. I'm glad you told me."

"I'm not sure there's much to be gained by going there."

"Maybe not, but it's on our way. We shouldn't ignore it."

"Okay," he said and started driving.

They were fifteen minutes from the college and passing a small private airstrip when a memory so strong, so poignant, had her clenching her stomach.

"What's wrong?" Cal asked immediately.

"Mia. Mia died in a plane crash."

"Okay." His voice was steady, which was good because she felt about ready to spiral right out of her body.

"Tell me about it," he said. He kept driving but she could tell that he reduced his speed, as if he was getting ready to pull over or stop suddenly if necessary.

"Her best friend's dad was a pilot. She frequently flew with them. They were going to their cabin at the lake one summer evening when their plane crashed. Mia, her best friend, both the parents. Everyone died upon impact."

He was silent for a few minutes.

She could feel herself get more in control.

"What was her friend's name?" he asked.

"Misty. It was always Misty and Mia. M&M, like the candy."

"What was Misty's last name?"

"Wagner. Misty Wagner." She shook her head. "How can I remember her best friend's name and I can't remember Mia's?"

He shrugged. "Easy. You probably heard your parents say a hundred times things like *make sure it's okay with the Wagners* or *the Wagners will drop Mia off later.* They probably never referred to Mia by her last name."

It made sense. Suddenly something else was making a lot of sense. "It was a plane crash. Four people died. It had to have made the papers. There has to be some record. If I can find that, I can find Mia's last name. I can find myself."

He nodded. "It's a possibility."

She hadn't surprised him and she realized that he'd been going down that path from the minute she'd said that her sister had died in a plane crash.

"Where did the crash occur?" he asked.

She thought. "I don't know. I'm not sure it's something that I've forgotten. It's possible that I never knew. At seven, it probably didn't matter to me. And my parents never talked about it."

"Where was the lake house?"

She shook her head. "On a lake?" she said, throwing both hands up in the air. It was so frustrating.

He smiled. "We can find it." He held out his phone.

"I hope so. I know the month and year of the crash and I'm pretty sure that Mr. Wagner was a big shot in business. He ran some company."

"What was his first name?"

"Steve. I think. Look, I know it's not much but I

think the crash got lots of press. I can remember my mother, years later, talking about what vultures some reporters could be. I guess a few camped out in our front yard, wanting a quote."

She opened the browser on the phone and searched. Nothing. Damn it. She'd been so sure.

After ten minutes, he said, "If it happened twenty-five years ago, then perhaps the news coverage was never in digital form. We may need to dig deeper, to actually look for a hard copy of an article. We should probably try the library in Kansas City."

She nodded. "It's worth a try. But not the public library. Let's go to the library at Moldaire College. The college is at the center of all of this. I know it. It's time to figure this out."

But before they got to the campus, Cal followed the directions on his GPS to Raftors. The lingerie shop was in a strip mall, on the very edge of the Moldaire campus. There were fast-food restaurants on both sides, with a vacuum cleaner repair store at one end and a cash store at the other end of the retail cluster.

There were thirteen cars in the parking lot. Once Cal shut off the car, she sat very quietly in her seat.

Cal stared at her, concern on his handsome face. "Maybe we should just forget this. You just had that memory of Mia and you're probably still a little shook. We're probably not going to get anything here anyway," Cal said.

"I've been here before."

"Really?" he said. "Just when I thought you couldn't surprise me anymore," he said.

"I have been in this parking lot. Sitting. Waiting."

"For who?"

She closed her eyes. "I don't know." She put her hand on the door. "Now I'm really glad we came. Maybe G got those matches from me."

"I guess that's a possibility. Do you think you might have come here with him?"

She shook her head. "I came here with someone. We were eating chicken fingers in the car." She turned to him. "Chicken fingers. How is it that I can remember something like that and I don't know who I was with?"

"I have no idea. Ready to go inside?"

She opened her car door in response. When she got close, she could see that Raftors was a small store, probably not bigger than twenty feet wide by thirty feet deep. When they opened the door, a bell tinkled. There was a woman behind the counter who looked up.

Even though it was spelled differently, Raftors might have gotten its name from the fact that there was merchandise all the way up to the rafters. Bras, bustiers, corsets and panties. Every color. Many materials. Even fur.

When they got to the counter, she saw that there was a glass bowl of matchbooks. She glanced at Cal. He shrugged.

The woman behind the counter was frowning at her. "I told you I'd call if Jessica came back into work. She hasn't. That's why I didn't call," the woman finished, her tone acidic.

She was so surprised that she was literally speechless. But that was okay because the woman wasn't done.

"I run a legitimate business here. And whatever Jessica has done, she did it on her own time. Not through me and not through this store."

She decided it was one of those times to go for broke.

She looked at the woman's name tag. "Marcy, I'm sorry to bother you. I was in an accident a few days ago. So, you have me at a slight disadvantage. You remember me but I don't remember you. I don't remember ever being in this store."

Marcy rested her crossed arms on her ample stomach. "So you've got…brain damage?"

She hoped not. "Temporary amnesia," she said. "Can you tell me who Jessica is?"

Marcy looked at Cal. "Who is he?"

"A friend who helped me after the accident. Jessica?"

"Jessica worked here, up until about two weeks ago. You came in here about a week ago asking for her. I told you the truth. She quit without notice and I didn't expect to see her. She never even came in to pick up her last check. You asked me if I would call you if she came back in. I said I would."

"Why did I want to talk to Jessica?"

The woman shook her head. "I ain't never had a conversation like this before. You said she was your sister and that you hadn't seen her for some time."

"Thank you. Ah…one last question, I promise. Did I tell you my name?"

"Yeah. You said it was Jean."

She looked at Cal to see if he had any other questions. He shook his head. She smiled at the woman. "Again, thank you. You've been very helpful."

They were three feet from the door when Marcy called out, "I hope you get your memory back. That has to be really weird."

"Really weird," she repeated when they were back in the car. "I'll tell you what's really weird. I don't have a sister named Jessica. I know that. Mia was my sister. My only sister. Yet, for some reason, I'm trying to find some woman, claiming that she's my sister." She slammed her hand against the dash. "I told that woman my name was Jean. My name isn't Jean. That's another lie. I know it."

"I don't know what I expected," Cal said, "but it wasn't that. I think you did the right thing by telling her the truth. Otherwise, you wouldn't have gotten anything out of her."

"I got something but it doesn't make any sense."

"It will," he said. "Let's go to Moldaire."

Chapter Sixteen

The college library was one of the formidable stone buildings on the square. Now the open green space in front of it was no longer snow-covered but rather snow-spotted. In many places, patches of grass were visible. It was almost forty-five degrees outside and the remaining snow was melting fast.

There were many more students walking around with lots of the female students wearing colorful rain boots so that they could stomp through the slush.

Her tennis shoes had gotten really wet walking across campus.

"I…"

"What?" Cal asked.

She had started to tell him about the tennis shoes, about having one more memory. But he was already skittish about them being on campus. She didn't want to give him a reason to demand that they get the heck out of there.

But this was Cal. She trusted him.

"Stormy?" he prodded.

"I…I just know we're going to find something," she said. She'd already told him that Moldaire felt familiar. She didn't need to tell him about walking across the campus in tennis shoes.

He studied her. But then he focused on parking the SUV.

They walked into the library. There were two people behind the circulation desk who didn't even look up as they passed. There was a big sign with arrows that directed library patrons to various sections.

To the right of the big sign was a bank of computers. "Let's try the computer first, just in case," he said.

He sat down at one, followed the directions to log in as a library guest and typed in *Steve Wagner plane crash*. Nothing came up. He typed in *Misty Wagner*. Nothing. She started to look around for someone to ask for assistance. Cal kept typing, trying search terms. Finally, he got it with *Stephen Wagoner*.

She had been mostly right, even though the name was just a little different. Stephen Wagoner had been a big enough deal that the *Wall Street Journal* had covered the story. They followed the link and started reading the three-paragraph story.

When Cal finished, he looked at her. She was re-reading the portion about the others who'd died in the crash. Mia Akina.

"That's her," she said.

Cal put his hands on the keyboard. "Ready?" he whispered.

She nodded.

He typed *Mia Akina obituary* into the search field.

In three more clicks, she was transported back twenty-five years and learning that Mia was dead. The pain ripped through her and she must have made some sound because Cal's arm went around her back.

"Steady," he said, his mouth close to her ear.

She drew in a deep breath. At almost the very end of the relatively short obituary was the information she'd been searching for. *Mia Akina is survived by her parents, Rafal and Jacinta Akina, and her seven-year-old sister, Nalana Akina.*

"Nalana," he said.

If she had been expecting an epiphany of sorts upon learning her name, she would have been bitterly disappointed. She felt no different.

"I guess," she said. Although when Cal had pronounced it with the accent on the second syllable and a soft *a*, it had seemed right. "I knew it wasn't Jean."

She read the remaining paragraph. *Rafal and Jacinta Akina, both sports journalists residing in Los Angeles, were in New York covering the US Open at the time of the plane crash.*

"Sports journalists. That explains a lot," Cal said.

"I'm not sure it matters," she said, unable to keep the disappointment out of her voice.

"Of course it matters," he said. "Every piece of information is a piece of you. It leads us to something else. Now we can easily find out where you live and where you work, Stormy. I mean, Nalana."

"For right now, let's just stick to Stormy. I'm getting used to it." She looked at her watch. "In less than twelve hours, it's going to be Saturday. We need to figure out why that's important."

"We—"

A blaring alarm drowned out anything else he might have said. Library users pushed back chairs, gathered books and started toward the entrance. "Fire," she said.

"Let's get out of here," Cal said. He did a couple

fast clicks to clear the browser history and then he shut down the computer. Then it was a fast but casual walk out the front entrance. People were milling outside the building, as if they anticipated it was simply an irritating drill rather than a full-blown emergency.

She didn't smell any smoke or see any fire so she assumed they might be right. Two campus police cars pulled up, sirens adding to the noise level. Two officers got out of each, two women, two men. As one of the men brushed past her, he gave her a look and might have stumbled just a little but then he kept on walking.

She and Cal got into their SUV. "Did you see that?" she asked. The brief interaction with the campus police officer had shaken her more than she'd expected.

"Uh-huh," Cal said. "I'm trying to decide if it was just a double take to look at a pretty woman or if it meant something. Is it possible that your concern about the police is because of some interaction with the campus police?"

"It's possible," she agreed. "What do you think we should do?"

"Maybe he recognized you because he's seen you around campus. No big deal. But if he recognized you because of some association with the Mercedes Men, then it's going to be relatively easy for them to look at the security camera tapes and realize that the two of us are together. That means G will no longer buy the story that I'm a crazy veteran chasing bad guys in the woods. The house won't be safe."

"I don't want to go back," she said. "I don't want anything bad to happen in that house. It's going to be Chase's home. Nobody needs those kinds of memories.

Plus, we need to be here. I can feel it. Something is going to happen. We need to be close to try to stop it."

"Let's get the hell out of here, at least," he said. "No sense making it easy for them. Where to?"

"We need to go back to The Blue Mango."

"Call them first. See if they are open." He tossed her his phone. He pulled out of the parking space and started driving.

She dialed. When the phone was answered on the second ring, she almost dropped it. "I was just calling to see if you were open," she said.

"Yes. Until ten tonight."

"Thank you," she said and ended the call. She turned to Cal. "Let's go."

IT WAS SIGNIFICANTLY more difficult to find a parking spot than it had been the day before. The Blue Mango was evidently a popular restaurant.

Cal finally found a spot a block away and they walked. He walked nearest to the street, keeping Stormy closer to the buildings. That provided some protection, although there could always be someone lurking in a doorway, ready to attack.

Danger could come from anywhere and for some reason, perhaps it was Stormy's certainty that something bad was going to happen on Saturday, he was running at full alert. The idea of something harming Stormy was eating at him, making his normal confidence feel shallow and cracked at the edges. He was this close to ignoring her insistence that the police couldn't be trusted. He wanted her protected.

He'd been trained by the best of Uncle Sam's navy to always consider all the possibilities. That meant that he couldn't ignore the possibility that Stormy was afraid of the police because she'd done something bad. Maybe at this very moment the police were hunting her. Was that why the campus cop had done a double take? Was her picture circulating because she was wanted?

What the hell would he do?

He knew the answer to that one.

Whatever it took to keep her safe. He had money saved. He could afford to hire a good attorney.

For now, he'd honor her wishes to stay away from the police. He could not take the risk that she'd be taken into custody and never forgive him for the betrayal.

When they got close, he motioned to Stormy to let him enter first. It wasn't gentlemanly but it was prudent.

The interior of The Blue Mango was filled with dark wood, black-and-white tiles and soft lighting. There were big plants in the entryway and a young man stood beside a high table that had two stacks of large, leatherbound menus.

Cal took a quick inventory. Bar off to his right. Oval. Stools on three sides. Sixteen seats. Two lone males, drinking beer. Male bartender. Four other patrons, split into two tables of two. Three empty tables.

Restaurant to his right, booths alongside the far wall, tables in the center, waitstaff station along the back wall. There was a family of four at one of the tables, and he could see the tops of heads in two booths. None of them had the jet-black hair that Golya sported.

"Two for dinner?" the young man asked. He had given Stormy a quick glance, the kind of look a guy gives an attractive woman, but Cal didn't see any flicker of recognition in his eyes.

Stormy stepped forward. "Yes. Could we have a table in the bar?"

"Of course," the young man said, reaching for two menus. He led them to one of the open tables.

When he left, Cal leaned forward. "Anything?" he asked.

Stormy nodded. "Maybe. It seemed very familiar when we walked in." She opened her menu. "Let's order," she said. "Maybe it will come to me."

Cal got a steak, Stormy got the salmon in a lemon butter sauce with capers. Both got baked potatoes and clam chowder to start. Neither one of them ordered a drink, choosing to stick with water instead.

They were halfway through their food when the bartender, on his way back to the bar with a tray of clean glasses, passed by their table.

"Hey, how's it going?" he said, looking at Stormy. "Nice to see you again."

Stormy smiled and the bartender kept walking. When he was behind the bar, Stormy leaned forward.

"He knows me."

Her voice was filled with hope and Cal was reminded of how frustrated she must be to be living in a void, not having the comfort of a past, an identity.

"Seems so," he said, cutting a piece of his steak with perhaps a little more force than necessary. The bartender was probably midtwenties and a good-looking guy. The idea that Stormy may have sat at the bar and flirted with him was not a happy thought.

"I think we're going to have an after-dinner drink at the bar," she said.

For the next five minutes, she pushed her salmon around on her plate. When the waiter came by, she gratefully gave it up. He offered dessert and they declined. Cal asked for the check and paid in cash once the waiter brought it.

"I think I should go to the bar alone," she said.

Like hell. "Why?" he asked.

She rolled her eyes. "You're…imposing. And I don't think that's going to encourage him to talk to me."

Tough. "What happened to the stepbrother story? That's what you told everybody else."

She shook her head.

He didn't like it. Not one bit. But she was probably right. She might be more successful in getting information if he wasn't there. He remembered his promise to never ask her to hide in the closet again. Damn.

He studied the windows, the angles. He pulled a twenty out of his pocket and slid it across the table. "Sit at the end stool. Order a drink. Keep it on your left side, far enough that I can see it from behind you. If at any time things start to go south, move it to your right side. I'll be there in thirty seconds."

She picked up the money. "Got it," she said. She stood up. He thought she was going to walk away without another word. Instead, she leaned forward and brushed a kiss across his cheek.

It might have been a familial good-night kiss that a woman reserved for a favorite stepbrother. But her lips were warm, her breath sweet and lemony, and she lingered just a moment too long. It was a kiss of reassurance, a kiss of promises. "Thank you," she whispered.

Cal walked out of the restaurant thinking that Stormy could probably ask him to stand naked in the middle of the street and flag down buses and he'd do it. He crossed the street and stood under the awning of a dry-cleaning

store that was closed. Through the far window, he could
see into the bar. Could see the back of Stormy as she
sat on the last stool.

Could see the bartender approach and smile.

He congratulated himself on not reaching for his gun.

SHE SLID ONTO the stool. She picked up the bar menu,
flipped to the Cordials and Liquors tab and scanned
the possibilities. None of them looked particularly ap-
pealing.

The bartender was busy filling an order for one of
the servers. She left with a tray of wineglasses and two
margaritas. "Thanks, Joe," she said.

The bartender gave one of the men at the bar another
beer. Then he headed toward her, a smile on his face.

She had to take the chance. "How's it going, Joe?"

"Good," he said. "I thought maybe your consulting
assignment had ended," he said, "when I didn't see you
and Tim here on Monday night. I know how he loves
the oysters."

Who the heck was Tim? "We got busy," she said.
"Just couldn't fit it in."

"That's good. Megan," he said, tossing his head in
the direction of the server who was taking drinks in the
bar area, "thought that you might have thrown us aside
in favor of Strawbridge Bay. She'd heard Tim talking
about the food there."

"We like it here better," she said.

"Well, you were probably wise not to come in. It was
crazy here. We had all our frozen drinks at half price. I
blew up two blenders." He put a napkin in front of her.
"Want your usual, Jean?"

Jean. Again, the mysterious Jean. Sure, she'd take

Jean's usual. She was going to have to start writing down her names to keep track of all of them. "Absolutely," she said, smiling. She pushed the twenty in his direction.

He took it and came back with a Bailey's on the rocks and nine dollars of change. He set the glass in front of her and she casually moved it to the left, beyond her body. Then she picked up the five, leaving the four ones on the counter. "Tim and I are working different hours right now and haven't seen much of each other. He hasn't been in?"

Joe shook his head. He picked up a knife and began slicing limes into wedges. "No, but there were some people in on...let me think, was it Wednesday? Yes, definitely Wednesday night because we were closed unexpectedly yesterday due to a little water problem. Anyway, they were asking about the both of you. Said they worked with you at Moldaire College. I guess I didn't realize that's where you and Tim were working. You know, I graduated from there."

"I guess we must not have mentioned it." People looking for her. It had to be the Mercedes Men. "Was it two men, both with dark hair?"

He shook his head. "No. Man and a woman. He had light brown hair and she was a blonde. Heavy on the makeup." He paused for effect. "I like the natural look myself," he said, his tone suggestive. "You do it well."

She smiled, really grateful that Cal wasn't here. He'd commandeer the knife and Joe would be missing a finger. "Hmm," she said, her mind whirling. Man and a woman. Coworkers. "You didn't happen to catch their names, did you?"

Joe stopped slicing. "I didn't. I think they left a card,

though. Asked me to give it to you if you came in."
He put down his knife. "I'm sure I threw it in the cash
register."

She could feel her heart start to beat fast in her chest.
This was it. The break that she'd been waiting for.

He opened the cash register and picked up the drawer
in the front, where they stuffed the larger bills. "It was
right here," he said. He kept looking.

Finally, he turned. "Sorry, Jean. Somebody else must
have thrown it away."

She tried to not let the disappoint swamp her. "Well,
if there are other consultants in town, I'd really like to
look them up. They didn't happen to mention anything
else, did they? Like maybe where they were staying?"

"No. But maybe I could take your number and if they
come back, give you a call."

"That would be great." She held out her hand and he
pulled a pen from behind his ear. She wrote Cal's cell
phone number on one of the bar napkins. He picked it
up and put it in his shirt pocket.

"I'm off next weekend," he said.

"Give me a call," she said. She felt bad leading him
on but she needed his help if the man and woman came
back to the bar looking for her.

"I thought maybe you were with that guy you were
having dinner with," Joe said.

"My stepbrother," she said. She'd have crossed her fingers if she was the superstitious type. "He's just visiting."

When she crossed the street, Cal discreetly motioned
for her to keep walking and he fell into step next to her.
"Well?" he said.

She told him about Jean and Tim and the strangers who were asking about them. He listened carefully. When they got to the car, he opened her door. Once he'd slid behind the wheel and pulled out, he said, "I saw him hand you a pen."

"I gave him your number," she said.

"My number?" he asked, turning his head.

"Well, he thinks it's mine," she said.

There was a pause. "Well, good. He's not my type."

She punched his arm. "Right now, I just want him thinking that he's Jean's type."

"So you and Tim have been frequenting this bar. And you've been going by the name of Jean. And you were coworkers."

"Yes. He referred to our consulting assignment. But why would I be using a false name for a consulting assignment? Why wouldn't Joe have known me as Nalana Akina. That's my name. We know that for a fact."

"Because maybe it's not your run-of-the-mill consulting assignment. It's something else. You're in this area for some other reason."

"But at the center of everything is Moldaire College. Joe said that he was surprised that Tim and I never mentioned that we were working at Moldaire. But the brown-haired man and blonde woman said we were coworkers at Moldaire." She shook her head. "This is impossible. How can I figure out my past when I'm lying to everyone?"

"I don't know. But your disappearance, and Tim's disappearance, have caused other people to start looking for you, to start asking questions. To be bold enough to leave a card. That's good."

"Maybe. I have two different groups of people looking for me. And I don't know why. And it's seven o'clock

on a Friday night and I think something bad is supposed to happen on Saturday. *Good* isn't the adjective
I would choose."

"It's a challenge," Cal conceded.

"We have to go to the Strawbridge Bay. Joe the bartender said that Tim told one of the servers that he liked
their food. Maybe Jean and Tim went there together.
Maybe the man and woman that are looking for Jean
and Tim will know to check there, too."

Cal tossed her his phone. "I hope it's close."

It was six miles away. The traffic was heavy and
it took twenty minutes to get there and another ten to
find a parking spot. They squeezed into one, between
a BMW and a Lexus. They watched the door for a few
minutes. "I think we're underdressed," she said.

"But our money is good," Cal countered. "I think
that's what they care about." He opened the car door
for her. "Are we eating again?" he asked as they walked
down the sidewalk.

"How about dessert and coffee?" she whispered.

It was smaller than The Blue Mango. Just one dining room with a service bar at the rear of the restaurant.
That was discouraging. There would be no talkative
bartender here.

"Table for two?" the young hostess asked. She could
not have been much more than sixteen.

"Yes." She looked directly at the girl and smiled.
The girl smiled back but showed no sign of recognition.
"We're just interested in your dessert menu."

"That's fine," the girl said.

She led them to a table in the middle of the restaurant. Cal sat so that he could see the door.

She looked around. No Mercedes Men. No brown-haired man or made-up blonde. Their server was a young black man who took their order for cheesecake and coffee politely but with no personal exchange.

"I have the craziest urge to stand up on the table and yell, does anybody here know me?"

"It's a bust," Cal said. "We had to try." He took a bite of his cheesecake. "And they have really excellent desserts."

"Thanks for trying to make me feel better," she said.

Cal finished his coffee. "We should get going. We have a long drive ahead of us."

"No. I don't want to go back to Ravesville. Let's go to Moldaire College instead. We can get a room in the student union."

"Did you forget that I wasn't even willing to have lunch there two days ago?"

"Nope. But it's different now. We have to stay close, where we can respond quickly. We aren't going to let G sneak up on us. And maybe they're not even here any longer. He's leaving the country. Maybe he's going to be long gone before whatever bad thing that's supposed to happen on Saturday actually occurs."

"The student union is a huge building. Difficult to secure even a small space. An attack could come from multiple directions," he said, still not convinced.

"There's no place better to stay. It's like hiding in plain sight." She was not going to back down.

He seemed to sense that. "Oh, what the hell," he said.

It took them forty minutes to drive back to the campus. It was now close to nine o'clock. They parked and walked into the pretty stone building. There was an imposing foyer with marble walls and intricately tiled flooring. Up four steps, to the left, there was a large restaurant that was open but didn't look busy, probably because it was past the dinner hour. In the middle was open space for students and visitors to gather. Lots of small groupings of chairs. The colors were soft in blues and violets, the lighting was good, and the overall effect was warm and comforting. There was a gas fireplace that was lit.

To the right was a big oak registration desk. They headed that direction and waited while the young man behind the desk finished his conversation. His name tag said Devon.

"We'd like a room," Cal told him once he'd hung up.

Devon started laughing. "You guys should buy some lottery tickets."

Huh?

Devon held up a hand. "Sorry. It's just that we've been sold out of rooms for a month. I've personally turned away at least thirty people today. But that call was to cancel a room. So I guess you guys can have it. I just need a name and a credit card."

"Mary Smith," she said. "And we'd like to pay with cash."

Devon nodded. "I guess that's okay. Hardly anyone does that anymore."

It took him another couple minutes of clicking computer keys before he picked up a plastic key card, ran it through a machine to activate it and handed it to them.

"Why is the student union so busy?" Cal asked.

"The game." The young man looked at them as if they were stupid.

"What game?"

Devon reached out an arm and pulled a newspaper off the stack at the end of the counter. It was the college newspaper. The headline read Secretary of State to Attend End of Season Game.

Her pulse started to race and she felt very warm.

She scanned the article quickly. Secretary of State Dane Morgan, who was an alumnus of Moldaire College and a fraternity brother to President LaTrope, would be the honored guest at Saturday's end-of-season game between Moldaire and rival Rollston College of Omaha, Nebraska. Following the game was a $200-a-plate, invitation-only dinner, emceed by Morgan to raise money for the college. LaTrope had promised that the dollars would go toward long-overdue repairs needed on the school's infrastructure.

"Cal," she said, her voice sounding strange to her own ears.

He leaned over her shoulder so that he could see what she was looking at. "Sounds like fun," he said nonchalantly. "Thanks," he said to Devon. Then he put his hand on her elbow and propelled her toward the elevator.

"Breathe," he whispered.

She wished it was that easy. She was dizzy and nauseous and her head felt as if it was going to split open. Her heart was pounding in her chest. She was going to pass out.

When the elevator door closed, she sagged against the wall.

"Hey," Cal said, putting his arm around her to support her. "What's going on?"

She gulped for air but it wasn't enough. Gulped again.

"Honey, you're hyperventilating," he said. With one arm around her, he cupped his other hand around her mouth. "Slow down."

"This is it," she managed. "Something bad…going to happen…secretary of state…at game."

The elevator dinged, indicating they'd reached the fourth floor. The door opened.

And in walked the Mercedes Men.

Chapter Seventeen

Cal did his best. But he'd lost a valuable second because his arms had been full of Stormy. But still he managed to take out two of them with quick sharp blows and he was going after the third one, Bad Knee, when the odds shifted quickly. He saw that G had Stormy's arms wrenched behind her back with the barrel of his gun resting against her neck.

"Don't hurt her," he said, putting his own hands in the air.

G said something in another language to the two men on the floor and they managed to get themselves up. Then, with one on each side of him, holding him tight, Bad Knee punched Cal in the face. It was a good swing.

As his head whipped back, he heard Stormy's cry. G barked out another order and they were moving fast down the hallway. Cal saw that one of the men had picked up the key card. He used it to unlock the room that had been assigned to Cal and Stormy.

He was pushed up against the wall and roughly searched. They tossed his phone to the floor and stepped on it, destroying it. Then they found his gun and they tossed it across the room before he took a hard hit to the right kidney. They flipped him back around and

Bad Knee got two more punches in, one to the face and one to the gut.

Then one of them, who was pretty good with a rope, yanked his arms back and tied his wrists together. Once he was tied, they shoved his head back, cracking it against the wall.

His two attackers took their positions, one on each side. They were being smart. Not taking it for granted that he'd be out of commission with his arms tied behind his back.

G still had his gun up against Stormy's neck. She looked frightened but he was grateful to see that she wasn't hysterical. She had pulled it together.

G leaned his face close to Stormy's. "You have caused me a great deal of trouble," he said. "I am not happy. And in my country, when a husband is not happy with his wife, he disciplines her." He motioned Bad Knee to approach. "Not her face," G said.

Bad Knee hit Stormy in the stomach, hard enough that he could have broken some ribs. Stormy's knees gave out but G held her up, until she managed to catch her breath.

Then G nodded and Bad Knee hit her again.

"That was for embarrassing me in front of my friends," G said. "They were expecting a wedding."

Fury, blind naked fury, swept through Cal. He was going to kill them all. Rip them apart with his bare hands.

Stay alive. Just stay alive until I can get us out of this. He willed the thought to her as finally Bad Knee stepped out of the way and he could make eye contact with her.

She gave him a weak smile then turned to G. "You're not my husband."

He pushed the barrel of the gun harder into her delicate neck. Using his free hand, he pulled at a chain around his neck. There was a silver ring with a wide band hanging on the chain. "I already wear your ring, my sweet. And soon you will wear mine."

Cal saw Stormy flinch and it was as if she could not take her eyes off the ring that G wore around his neck. She looked across the room to Cal. "That was Mia's. My grandmother gave it to her before she died. I got it when Mia died."

"Silence," G ordered. "You need to learn, even if it's the hard way, that I'm nobody's fool. Your partner already learned that lesson."

At first, Cal thought G was talking about him. But then he saw something cross Stormy's face and realized that he was wrong. G was talking about someone else. Stormy's partner.

It had to be the person that Stormy had said she couldn't remember but the emotion connected to the person made her sad. He could tell that Stormy was remembering exactly what had happened and it was something horrible.

G either wasn't as perceptive or he didn't care. He yanked on Stormy's arm and dragged her to the bed in the middle of the room. Then shoved her hard so that she fell upon the mattress.

She quickly scooted up, so that she was sitting with her back against the headboard.

Cal could tell the movement hurt her newly injured ribs. They would pay for that. Slowly.

There were tears in her eyes but he didn't think it

was because of her injuries. She was remembering and it was painful.

"Your plan is full of holes," she said.

G laughed. "I don't think so. Our bomb is already in place. The timer is ticking. What's the line?" he paused for effect. "That's right. Bombs bursting in air. Right about the time they're singing your disgusting national anthem, they'll get to experience the real thing."

The men in the room giggled as if they were thirteen-year-old girls.

Cal was confident that Stormy hadn't remembered or hadn't ever known about the bomb. Her comment about the plan had been a trick to get G to reveal more. She was brilliant.

"I will admit that you and your partner were an un-expected complication. Bad timing," he said, "on your part."

"Very," she said. "But we were able to get word to others. They know."

"Oh, I don't think so, my dear. As I expected, your people came nosing around, with some crazy story that that were trying to find you because an elderly relative had died. It was obvious that they were looking because you and your partner hadn't checked in as expected. I had to play the role of the trusted yet perplexed super-visor who didn't have a clue why you hadn't shown up for your job on the office cleaning crew. While all the time, I wanted to strangle every single person who asked a question about you and say, I want her just as badly as you do."

With his gun still pointed at Stormy, he motioned toward the remaining rope that was on the floor. Bad Knee picked it up, then roughly jerked first one arm, then the other, tying them to the headboard corner posts. Then he yanked on her legs, pulling her onto her back. He frowned at the boots she wore. He unzipped them and tossed them both aside. Then he tied each ankle to a footboard post.

She was spread-eagle on the bed. Fully clothed still but in the most vulnerable position a woman could be in. They wanted to humiliate her.

But damn her, she kept her chin in the air. *Take your best shot.* That was what her attitude said.

He'd never loved her more.

"I'll admit," G said, "you were more difficult to find than I expected. A woman in a wedding dress is easy to remember but no one seemed to know." He turned to Cal. "You were quite convincing, Mr. Hollister. You might have had a future in the movies that you Americans love so much."

Cal was rapidly clicking through the information that G was spewing out. *Your people came nosing around.* He'd been right. Stormy was in some kind of law enforcement, probably working undercover. *I had to play the role of the trusted yet perplexed supervisor who didn't have a clue why you hadn't shown up for your job on the office cleaning crew.* Stormy's disjointed memories made perfect sense. She'd been dressed in blue pants and a blue polo shirt. That was likely the uniform that the cleaning crew wore. But she'd remembered working on the computer for hours every night. She'd probably been documenting a case file or reporting information back to a superior.

But why had she been on the Moldaire College campus? Who had she been investigating? And how did that person figure into all of this?

Was it G that she'd been investigating? Somehow, Cal didn't think so. G had said something earlier that it had been bad timing on her part. Had she stumbled into something and before she could report it up the food chain, she and her partner had been captured?

He needed G to keep talking so that he could piece it together but G was evidently done with that. He motioned at Cal's two guards and suddenly they were pulling him toward the small bathroom. The student union had been built many years before and while the bathrooms might have been remodeled, some of its original *charm*, in the form of old fixtures, still existed. They pushed him onto the floor, tied his ankles together and then tied him to the thick steel leg of the pedestal sink.

He was sure they intended to kill him before it was all over. But for whatever reason, they were waiting. He suspected that G was still hoping for some cooperation from Stormy and if he killed Cal now, that wasn't likely to happen.

He was surprised they hadn't gagged him.

But then he understood why when Bad Knee came up behind him and he felt the sharp prick of a needle in his arm. "I gave him enough to knock a horse out," Bad Knee said to someone.

He heard G laughing.

Damn was his last thought.

SHE WOKE UP feeling sick, just like before, and the memory of what had happened swamped her. She hurt and it was difficult to take a deep breath. The room was dark and she wondered if it was nighttime but then realized that the shades had been pulled down and the curtains closed tight.

"Cal," she called out. Her voice was weak, barely a whisper. She swallowed hard. "Cal," she said louder.

Had they killed him? The thought paralyzed her. She loved him. It was like losing Mia all over again but this time with the knowledge that it was her fault. She'd dragged Cal into this mess.

She was going to make G and his friends pay.

For Cal. For Bolton, the best partner she'd ever had.

"Help," she yelled. "Help." Over and over again, until her voice was hoarse. But no one came. She cursed the century-old plaster walls and thick wood door that kept sound in.

She had to get free. And keep the secretary of state from getting blown up along with twenty-five thousand other football fans.

She pressed her rear into the mattress. There it was. In her pocket. The knife that Cal had given her.

They'd searched Cal but hadn't thought to search her. Now she needed to figure out how to get it out of her pocket and use it to free herself.

She pushed her rear against the mattress, trying to push the knife up. Again and again. It was painstakingly slow progress and she was sweating with the effort by the time the knife was finally free.

Now came the hard part. If she could get the knife up to one of her hands, she had a chance of gripping it in her fingers and sawing through the rope.

But how the hell was she going to get the knife anywhere near her fingers? And then she thought of Cal. She could not let him have died in vain.

She pulled again at all of her ropes. She twisted her wrists and her ankles, testing to see if there was any give. Nothing with her wrists. But maybe, the right ankle. She had good flexibility and strength in her ankles and feet. She needed to use that to her advantage.

She twisted her foot, back and forth, desperately trying to stretch the rope around her ankle. The braiding dug into her skin, cutting into her. It hurt but she kept going. It was her only chance.

It seemed to take forever but finally, the rope seemed loose enough. She flexed her foot downward, pushing it to an angle that it wasn't ever meant to go. But when she smoothly pulled her knee up, her foot slipped through the rope.

One leg was free. She lifted her head off the pillow. The skin around her ankle was bloody and raw but none of that mattered. With the use of a leg, she could do a lot.

"Cal," she said again, her poor voice spent. There was no answer, not even a rustle from the bathroom.

She had never felt so alone. It was even worse than the first time the Mercedes Men had taken her.

But Cal would not expect her to give up. He'd expect her to keep going. To be optimistic. "Half-full," she whispered. "My damn glass is half-full," she said.

She used her rear to push the knife down, toward the foot of the bed. When she got it as far as it would go, she bent her knee, bringing her foot as close to her rear as possible, and picked up the knife with her toes.

The sweet rush of success fueled her. She had a ways to go but she'd come further than the Mercedes Men could have ever contemplated.

Now came the tough part. She raised her leg, the knife clenched between her toes. She was going to have to toss it across her body and have it land close enough that her fingers could grab it.

It was going to have to be a perfect throw.

If she overshot, the knife would be on the floor. Might as well be on the moon. If she undershot, it would be just as frustrating. She'd be able to see it but it would be in a spot that she wouldn't be able to reach, even with one free leg. There was a limit to the amount of flexibility she had.

She judged the angle, the distance, took a deep breath and tossed it. It bounced off her hand and would have clattered to the floor if she hadn't been able to snag it at the last second. She turned it in order to get to the button. She pushed it and the blade extended.

She bent her hand at more than a ninety-degree angle at the wrist and set about the business of sawing through one of the ropes. It was tedious and her fingers cramped but she hung on to the knife and kept going.

And finally, one wrist was free. She pulled it down, wincing at the pain in her shoulder from having her hands pinned above her head for hours.

How many hours she had no idea. She didn't have a watch and there was no clock in the room, not even an alarm clock on the bedside table.

She needed to untie her other wrist. This was easier and in just minutes both wrists were free. Then she cut the final rope on her left foot. She was groggy, sick to her stomach, bleeding, and felt as if she'd been run over by a truck.

But there was no time to waste.

She stumbled her way into the bathroom. Cal was on the floor. Tied.

She knelt down. Felt for a pulse. It was there. Slow but steady. He was alive. Her heart soared with the knowledge.

The two of them needed to get out of there before the Mercedes Men came back.

She shook him. Hard. No response.

"Cal," she pleaded. "You have to help me."

Wildly, she looked around the bathroom. The bathtub was an old one, with claw feet and a shower curtain that wrapped all the way around it. She pulled it back. Saw the pipe for the shower and the showerhead on the hose.

She grabbed it, turned the cold water on full blast and aimed it at Cal's face.

Chapter Eighteen

Cal sputtered and spit. He was being water-boarded.

He must have been captured. They could try but they weren't going to get anything from him.

It took him a full minute before he realized that he was lying on the bathroom floor of the student union and Stormy was next to him, tears running down her face.

She was also trying to drown him.

"Wake up, damn you," she said. "Wake up."

"It would be helpful, darling, if you'd get that hose out of my face."

She dropped it and the clang seemed to echo through the small room. She fell on him. Hugging. Crying.

"It's okay," he said. "Now get this rope off me."

She efficiently sawed through the rope and the minute it was loose, he pulled his arms free. Even with the cold shower, he felt fuzzy and light-headed, as if he'd gone days without sleeping.

He looked at his watch. Hell. It was more as if he'd been sleeping for days. It was just after eleven. He'd been asleep for almost twelve hours. G and his merry men had shot him up with a massive cocktail.

He sat up. Reached out and gently touched her ribs. "Are you okay?"

She nodded.

Then he saw her bloody ankle and heel. "What the hell happened?" he asked.

"It's nothing. We have to get out of here before they come back." She started to cut through the ropes on his ankles. "Listen, Cal, I don't have time to explain but I'm an FBI agent."

"Figured something like that. What were you doing here at the college?"

"A clerk in the college accounting department had discovered that something looked odd with the financials. There was over two million dollars missing. She followed the trail as far as she could and she was confident that it was someone of substantial authority because money had been transferred from account to account and not everyone could do that. She went to her supervisor, who contacted the FBI. Bolton and I were sent undercover. Because we didn't know whom we could trust at the college, we told no one. We applied for jobs and the only open positions at the time were on the cleaning crew. That was perfect in that it gave us access to every executive's office at the college."

She made a final swipe with the knife and his ankles were free. He stood up and gripped the edge of the sink for support.

"I was Jean and Bolton was Tim. Even when we went to dinner on our off time, we stayed in those personas. We drove into Kansas City, thinking the distance between there and Moldaire reduced the likelihood that anybody would recognize us. He took that picture of me at The Blue Mango. It was on my cell phone. G must have gotten it off of it when he took it from me after Bolton and I were captured."

"What's missing money have to do with a bomb in the stadium?"

She put her arm around him, as if she was afraid that he was going to fall down. He didn't shake it off because it felt good to touch her.

"We didn't know anything about a bomb." She shook her head. "Trust me on this, I'm not the agent they would have sent. As it turns out, I'm not an accountant but close. My specialty is white-collar crime, specifically embezzlement. It took weeks but my partner and I were able to access most of the information we needed. Some if it was hard copy. That was easy. People who have locked offices rarely lock up information in their offices. The computer records that we needed were harder to get but not too hard." She looked up at him. "You'd be amazed at how many executives write their passwords on a scrap of paper and stick it under their keyboards. While we were supposed to be cleaning their offices, we would access the computer, copy off all activity on a thumb drive and analyze it back at our hotel."

Cal walked out of the bathroom and over to the window. He moved the shade and curtain just a fraction of an inch and looked outside. The room was still whirling but it was slowing down. "People are heading to the stadium. We have to get out of here, get to the police. Where do they fit in this?"

"I think the real police are fine. It was the campus police that my subconscious knew we couldn't trust. My partner and I had decided that we needed to get into the president's office. We had eliminated most everyone else as suspects and there was a paper trail that was leading to the president's office. He's married but had a young girlfriend."

"Let me guess. Jessica from the lingerie store." He did a couple deep knee bends to get the circulation moving in his legs.

"Yeah. Several hundred thousand dollars had been transferred into her account. And suddenly she was missing. There was no evidence that she was harmed. I think she basically got what she wanted from the guy and booked it out of here."

"What did you find in the president's office?"

"More than we should have. We were inside when we heard someone outside. We hid in the closet." She gave him a quick smile. "I know. A closet. Anyway, people came in. I recognized the one voice. It was G, who was the supervisor of the cleaning crew. From day one he'd made my skin crawl, always looking at me, brushing up against me. We didn't recognize the other voice but soon it was clear that it was the president. G was blackmailing him. Giving him money so that he could pay back what he'd stolen from the college. In exchange, the president had invited his friend and former fraternity brother, the secretary of state, back for the end-of-the-season football game. I remember being really angry that they were going to use a sporting event as the venue."

"G is a terrorist. So is the president of the college."

"Yes. They never talked about a bomb. We assumed that they were going to shoot the secretary. Anyway, after they left, my partner and I got the hell out of there. But what we didn't realize was that the office was being watched by a campus police officer on G's payroll. We left, he followed and tried to apprehend us. He killed

Bolton. I'm not sure he meant to or if his gun went off accidentally. Anyway, he took me hostage. They retrieved the computer from Bolton's hotel room. Our transmissions were always secure but they evidently got enough to realize that we were federal agents. I think that might have been when the plan to go back to Russia got hastily thrown together. I have no idea why a real wedding was necessary."

Cal was looking for his gun that they'd tossed aside. He looked up. "Pride, Stormy. To a man like G, pride is important. He wanted his friends to believe that he was marrying a very beautiful woman." His gun was gone. He'd expected as much.

He grabbed her boots and tossed them to her. "Stormy, you need to contact your people so that they can get the local police involved. They're going to have to mobilize very quickly to make sure the secretary of state is in a safe spot and get everyone away from the stadium."

"What are you going to do?"

He cracked open the door of the room and looked down the hallway. It was empty. He looked back over his shoulder and smiled at her. "I'm going to see if I can figure out how to shut down that bomb."

THEY TOOK THE elevator down to the registration desk. After doing a quick check to make sure they didn't recognize anybody in the lobby, they approached the desk.

"We have an emergency," she said to the clerk, this time a young woman. "I'm an FBI officer and I need to use your phone."

The woman didn't even ask to see any identification.

Just got off the stool she'd been sitting on and stepped away from the desk. There was a second empty stool and draped over it was a black jacket. There was a college ID badge pinned to the pocket.

"Whose jacket is that?" Cal asked.

"My supervisor's. He stepped away for just a minute."

Cal picked it up and put it on. It was a little small and the picture didn't look anything like him. She looked closer at the badge. Geoff Larkin, Manager.

"You can't take that," the clerk said.

"She will explain," Cal said, his voice polite.

She felt his hand on her shoulder. Cal leaned in and gave her a hard kiss. "No heroics," he said. "Promise me."

"You're the one going off to disarm a bomb," she said.

"I have to," he said simply. "I love you, Stormy," he added, already moving. "And I'm going to marry you and you're gonna wear that pretty ivory dress you saw in the wedding dress shop."

Then he was out the door.

The desk clerk was staring at her, her mouth open. "Wow," the woman said.

Wow, indeed.

She pressed her hand over her mouth. She wanted to call him back, to make him promise to stay by her side. But Cal Hollister had been a soldier, one of the best of the best. He could not sit back and wait while a terrorist killed innocent bystanders. She could not ask him to do that.

She needed to do her part. She went behind the counter, picked up the phone and started dialing.

CAL HAD SEEN his share of bombs over the years and had a pretty good idea of how he'd engineer a large explosion in a football stadium. Explosives would have to be planted at multiple locations and tripped simultaneously by an electric charge. He needed to find the source of that charge. It was possible that there could be multiple sources but that heightened the possibility of discovery. He was betting on one.

And he was betting that it was in an area that most people never saw. An area that was off-limits to most people but not to the maintenance personnel. The area under the stadium.

When he got to the stadium, he didn't hesitate. He walked to the front of the line, vaulted over the turnstile and flashed his badge with his thumb partially over the picture in the direction of the kid taking tickets.

"Manager Geoff Larkin. We've got a water problem," he said and kept walking. In the distance, he heard the sounds of approaching sirens. Lots of them.

Good. Stormy had made her call.

And there was no doubt a bomb squad in Kansas City. But it would take them a little bit to mobilize. They'd want to look at blueprints. They'd need to debate the options. The preferred method was never to have an actual person defuse the bomb. They'd want to send a robot in to remove the bomb and transfer it to a safe location to deal with it there. Dealing with it could take the form of a robot defusing it, letting it detonate in a controlled environment or even taking their own bomb to blast this one to hell.

They'd act according to protocol and that was all well and good in certain circumstances but protocol took time, and that was one thing he was confident they didn't have.

He found the freight elevators and got in. There were two lower levels, B1 and B2. Damn it. Two levels meant it would take twice as much time to search.

He stabbed B1 and prayed that he was right.

He would have felt much better with his gun. All he had was the knife that he'd given to Stormy. The knife had already come in very handy earlier today. It would have to be enough.

The door opened and he stayed inside the elevator. Edged his head out. He didn't want to meet up with any of the Mercedes Men if he didn't have to. They would slow him down.

The floor and walls were cement, the ceiling was a mass of white PVC pipes and encased electrical wiring. There were wire-fronted storage units, probably ten feet wide, against one wall. Some were filled with cardboard boxes, one had stacks of yellow cones and a pile of orange flags, one had what appeared to be brand-new toilets. On the other side of the room were two big rooms. Meeting spaces.

He closed his eyes. Breathed deep.

Then he stepped back into the elevator. He was going lower.

The B2 level looked a little like the floor above it in that it was all gray cement. But in the middle of the large space was a fully enclosed structure.

The power plant.

He could hear the hiss and crack of big boilers that were heating water that would ultimately supply heat and more to the upper levels. He tried to open the door. It was locked.

Damn it.

Then he saw the badge reader next to the door. His only hope was that the security processes at Moldaire weren't overly sophisticated and that all management personnel had access to all areas of the campus. He ripped Geoff Larkin's badge off his coat and slid it through the narrow channel.

He heard the click, grabbed the door and was inside.

It was a sea of commercial boilers, huge generators and chillers. He glanced at his watch. Time was running out. He had to find the power source and find it fast.

On his second loop around the room, he saw it. A small box, taped to the underside of one of the boilers, with a wire leading up to the ceiling and then beyond. He squatted down and used the edge of his knife to flip open the metal box.

He examined the three wires, all the same color. Why was it in the movies they always made it look easy by having a red, white and a green wire. And the guy always had somebody on the phone, walking him through the process. *Now cut the red one.*

He had nobody. And no way of knowing how much time he had left. In the movies, there was always a ticking clock. Not one here. All he knew was that the national anthem was sung at the very beginning of the game. Which had to be just about now.

He pulled all three wires at the same time.

Chapter Nineteen

After she had contacted her supervisor, things had moved quickly. The man had quickly called in both local and state police departments. He'd also reached out to one of the agents who'd been dispensed to Moldaire earlier in the week, looking for Nalana and Bolton. Within minutes, that male agent had arrived, moved her to the manager's office that was behind the registration desk and stood guard at the door.

She'd begged to go to the stadium but her supervisor had expressly forbidden it. Nalana was to stay put until the terrorists could be apprehended. She'd hated that she knew he was right. She wanted to be with Cal but she could not take the chance that the Mercedes Men would somehow intercept her and she'd be in a position of being a bargaining chip that might allow the terrorists to escape.

And Cal had said no heroics. She owed it to him to be careful, to be here when he came back.

She had just started to dial the phone to express her condolences to Bolton's family when she heard the explosion. She sank down in the chair and dropped the receiver. It hit the desk with a thud.

The bomb had gone off. It was unthinkable.

She'd been so confident that Cal would be able to do it, that he would come back to her in one piece, with his slightly cocky attitude and his killer grin. She hadn't allowed herself to contemplate any other option.

But the explosion had to mean that he had not been successful. And she quite frankly had no idea how she would bear it.

She put her face in her hands. Her head, her heart, her whole body felt heavy, as if she would never again have the strength to lift it. *Oh, Cal. I did so love you.*

She would have to call his brothers and tell them that Cal had died a hero, trying to save innocent people. She remembered the day that he'd been insistent that she memorize their numbers. He'd done it to ensure that she wouldn't be left defenseless or without resources. She would tell Chase how much Cal had loved him, how he had known the sacrifices that Chase had made for him and how he'd come to terms with that knowledge over the years, and how he'd challenged himself to be the kind of person who could act in the same selfless manner.

She could stay to help them with the funeral. And the people would come and point to her and wonder whether she was somebody important in Cal Hollister's life.

And she would try to find some comfort in knowing that while their time together had been short, they had connected in a way that most people never had the joy of experiencing. It had been brief but it had been love.

And she would wrap that around her for the cold days that were sure to come. It would take time but in his memory, she would make sure her glass was half-full again. "I will," she whispered.

"Will what?"

Her head whipped up. Cal. Sweet, sweet Cal. She leaped up from behind the desk and ran to him. He held out his arms, she jumped and wrapped her legs around him. She gripped his face in her hands. "I thought you were dead," she said. "I heard the explosion."

"I'm harder to kill than that." He held her tight. "They had a second, much smaller bomb, in the president's office. It's trashed but nobody was in the building. No casualties there. No explosion or casualties at the stadium. The secretary of state is in his car, on the way back to the airport."

He said it as if it was no big thing. All in a day's work. He was amazing. "What about G and the others?"

The agent who'd been at the door was smiling. "I don't want to intrude but I just heard. Golya Paladis and his comrades have been apprehended on their way to a small airport outside of Kansas City."

Cal held up a finger. "Golya is wearing a silver ring on a chain around his neck. We want it back."

"I'll see to it," the agent said. "We also have word that a campus police officer has just surrendered outside of the stadium. The president of the college was picked up at his house."

It was over. She leaned her forehead against Cal's lips. "Now what?"

"Now we go shopping. Let's get that wedding dress on order or whatever crazy thing we need to do to ensure that it's here and ready for you within a couple weeks. That's all the longer I'm waiting."

"If it's not here on time, I'll wear your T-shirt and sweatpants."

He smiled. "Okay by me. They're easy to get off."

* * * * *

You'll find more books in Beverly Long's
RETURN TO RAVESVILLE *miniseries in 2016!*

Read on for a sneak preview of
LUCKY SHOT,
the third book in
THE MONTANA HAMILTONS
by New York Times *bestselling author*
B.J. Daniels

MAX MADE A few calls to see what kind of interest there was in the photos of Senator Buckmaster Hamilton with his first wife, the back-from-the-dead Sarah Johnson Hamilton. There was always skepticism with something this big. But not one of the people he called told him to get lost.

"Where can you be reached?" they each asked in turn. "I'll have to get back to you… Is there any chance of getting an exclusive if these photographs…?" The questions came.

Not one to count his chickens before they hatched, Max still couldn't help feeling as if the money was already in his pocket. He could already taste the huge steak he planned to have as soon as he got Kat Hamilton to verify that the photos he'd taken were of her long-lost mother.

Then it was just a matter of waiting for the calls to start coming in and the bidding to begin. All he had to do was wait around until four for Kat.

He'd parked his pickup down the street, so he could watch the art gallery and see who came and went. A little after four, he spotted Kat Hamilton. She looked just as she had in her photo on her website. He watched her climb out of a newer model SUV, pull a large folder from the back and head across the street toward the gallery.

As he got out of his pickup, he admitted that he was flying by the seat of his pants. He wasn't sure how he was going to play this. He just hoped that the Max Malone charm didn't let him down. Passing a shop window, he caught his reflection and stopped to brush back his too-long hair. He really needed a haircut, and a shave wouldn't hurt either, he thought as he rubbed a palm along his bristled jaw.

Well, too late for any of that. He straightened his shirt, sniffed to make sure he didn't reek—after all, he'd spent the night sleeping under the stars in the back of his truck. He smelled like the great outdoors, and from what he could tell, Kat Hamilton might appreciate that. Most of her photographs he'd seen were taken in the great outdoors.

Still, he knew this wasn't going to be easy. Kat Hamilton wasn't just a rich, probably spoiled artist. She was a rich, probably spoiled artist whose daddy was running for president and whose birth mother was possibly unstable. He had no idea what it was going to take to get what he wanted from the unapproachable Kat Hamilton.

When he pushed into the gallery, the bell over the door chimed softly and both women turned in his direction. The gallery owner looked happy to see him. Kat? Not so much. He saw her take in his attire from his Western shirt to his worn jeans and boots. He'd left his straw cowboy hat in the truck, but his camera bag was slung over one shoulder.

"This is the man I was just telling you about," the shop owner said.

Kat's gray eyes seemed to bore into him as he sauntered toward her. Mistrust and something colder made her gaze appear hard as granite. She was dressed in an oversize sweater and loose jeans, that approach-at-your-own-risk look welded on her face.

"Max Malone," he said, extending his hand. "I'm a huge fan of your work, but I'm sure you hear that all the time."

Her handshake was firm enough. Her steely gaze never warmed, just as it never left his. "Thank you." Her voice had an edge to it, a warning. *Tread carefully.*

"I was especially taken with your rain photo," he said, moving in that direction, hoping she would take the hint and follow.

"You should show him your latest ones you brought in today," the gallery owner said.

Kat didn't jump at that.

"Would you mind if I took a photo of this? I want to show it to my wife. This would be perfect for her office."

"That would be fine," Kat said, clearly not invested in his company. He was reminded that she came from a wealthy family. She didn't need to make money from her photographs.

He snapped the shot of her rain photo and then walked back to where he'd left her standing. Every line of her body language said she'd had enough of him. He felt as if he was chipping away at solid ice. Charm wasn't going to get what he wanted. He hoped he wouldn't be forced to buy one of her photographs. The prices were a little steep, and he doubted cash would warm her up.

He was tempted, though, to buy the one she'd taken of the pouring rain. There was something about the shot... "I hate to even show you the photo I took," he said, stopping next to her to show her a scenery shot he'd taken on his camera while he'd been waiting for her to show up at the gallery.

She gave the photo a cursory glance and started to turn away when he flipped to the one he believed to be of her mother.

Kat Hamilton froze. Her gaze leaped from the camera to him. She took a step back, her gray eyes sparking with anger.

"I'm sorry," he said innocently, even though he felt a surge of pleasure to see some emotion in her face. "Is something wrong?"

"Who are you?" she demanded. "You're one of those reporters who have been camped outside the ranch like vultures for weeks."

That pretty well covered it, while at the same time confirming what he already knew. The photo was of Sarah Hamilton.

"I guess I don't have to ask you if the woman in the photo is your mother," he said as he put his camera away.

"Do you want me to call the police?" the shop owner asked as she stood wringing her hands.

"No, this man is leaving," Kat said, glaring poison darts at him. She looked shaken. Clearly, he'd caught her flat-footed with the photo.

"For what it's worth, I really do like your photos." With that he left. She hurled insults after him. Not that he didn't deserve them.

He was just doing his job. He doubted Kat Hamilton had ever had a real job. But even though he could and would defend his to the death, he was always sorry when innocent people got hurt.

It was debatable how innocent Sarah Hamilton was at

this point, though. Unfortunately, her daughters would pay the price for her notoriety.

MAX HAD PLANNED to drive back to Big Timber. But as he crossed Main Street, he realized that he was starving. His productiveness had left him ready to call it a day. Stopping at a hotel with a restaurant on the lower level, he decided he'd stay in Bozeman for the night. He was about to leave his camera bag and laptop in his pickup, but changed his mind.

He knew he was being paranoid, but just the thought of someone breaking into his pickup, and stealing them and the photos on them, made him take the equipment with him. Earlier at Big Timber Java, he'd put the photos on a thumb drive and stuck it in his pocket. Still, he didn't want to take any chances.

He'd just sat down in the restaurant after getting a room, when the calls began coming in. He let them go to voice mail. He'd go through them in his room later. If he seemed too anxious it would make him look as if he didn't have the goods. He'd just ordered the restaurant's largest T-bone steak with the trimmings when he saw a pretty brunette sitting alone at a table perusing a menu.

She looked around as if a little lost. They made eye contact. She smiled, then put down her menu and got up to walk over to him. "I know this is going to sound forward…" She bit her lower lip as if screwing up her courage. "I hate eating alone and I've had this amazing day." She stopped. "I'm sorry. I'm sure you'd prefer—"

"Have a seat. I've had a pretty amazing day myself."

All her nervousness seemed to evaporate. "Thank you. I've never done anything like that before. I'm not sure what came over me," she said as she took a seat across from him. "It's just that I noticed you were alone and I'm alone…"

The woman looked to be a few years younger than his thirty-five years. After the day he'd had, he was glad to have company to celebrate with him.

"Max Malone," he said, holding out his hand.

"Tammy Jones." Seeing what was going on, the waitress set up cutlery at the table and took her order.

Tammy explained that she was a retail buyer for a local department store. She was in town visiting from Seattle. "I'm only in town tonight. I normally don't invite myself to a stranger's table. But I'm tired of eating alone and today I got a great raise. I feel as if I just won the lottery."

He told her he was on vacation and just passing through town. He'd found when he told anyone that he was a reporter, it made them clam up, too nervous that they might end up in one of his articles.

"I saw your camera bag. So what all do you shoot?" she asked, leaning toward him with interest.

"Mostly scenic photos," he said. "It's just a hobby." He didn't want to talk about his job. Not tonight. He didn't want to jinx it.

Their meals came, and they talked about movies, books, food they loved and hated. It was pleasant, so he didn't mind having an after-dinner drink with her at the bar. She had a sweet, innocent face, which was strange because she reminded him a little of Kat Hamilton, sans the gray eyes. He kept thinking of those fog-veiled eyes. Kat was a woman who kept secrets bottled up, he thought.

"Am I losing you?" Tammy Jones asked, touching his hand.

"No." He gave her his best smile.

"You seemed a million miles away for a minute there."

"Nope." Just at the gallery across the street where he'd seen a light on in the back. Was Kat Hamilton still over there? She'd brought in new photos, if that large flat portfolio she'd been carrying was any indication. He wished now that he'd asked to see them before he'd gotten thrown out.

"I know it's awful, but I'm not ready to call it a night." She met his gaze with a shy one. "A drink in my room?"

How could he say no? They took the stairs to her room on the second floor.

What could one more drink hurt? With a feeling of euphoria as warm as summer sunshine, he reminded himself of the photos he would be selling tomorrow.

When he woke the next morning, he was lying in the alley behind the hotel. While he still had his wallet, his camera and laptop were gone.

As he stumbled through the stupor of whatever he'd been drugged with, Max tried to figure out who'd set him up. He knew why he'd been so stupid as to fall for it. He'd wanted someone to celebrate with last night. As much as he loved his job, he got lonely.

Now, though, he just wanted his camera and laptop and the photos on them back. Maybe Tammy Jones— if that had even been her real name—had just planned to pawn them for money. But he suspected that wasn't the case once he checked his wallet and found he had almost a hundred in cash that she hadn't bothered with.

His head cleared a little more after a large coffee

at a drive-through. He put in a call to the department store where Tammy Jones said she worked as a buyer, hoping he was wrong. He was told no one by that name worked for the company, not in Bozeman, not in Seattle.

He groaned as he disconnected. Whoever the woman had been last night, she had only one agenda. She was after the photos.

But how did she even know about them? He'd made a lot of calls yesterday and quite a few people were aware that he had the shots. All the people he'd called, though, he'd worked with before and trusted them. That left... No way was that woman from the restaurant hired by the senator to steal the photos. If the future president had known about the photos he would have tried to buy them if not strong-arm him, Max was sure.

That left Kat Hamilton.

He drove back downtown. It was early enough that the gallery wasn't open yet, but the light was still on in the back. He parked on Main Street and walked down the alley. The rear entrance in the deserted alley had an old door and an even older lock. One little slip of his credit card, and he was inside, thankful for his misspent youth.

The first thing he saw was a sleeping bag in one corner of the back area with a battery-operated lamp next to it and a book lying facedown on the floor. The woman clearly didn't appreciate the spines of books.

He found Kat wearing a pair of oversize jeans and a different baggy sweater. Clearly, this must be the attire she preferred. But he thought about bottled up secrets. Was she hiding under all those clothes? She stood next to a counter in the framing room of the gallery, her back to him, lost in her work. "I want my camera and laptop back."

At the sound of his voice, she spun around, gray eyes wide as if startled but not necessarily surprised. If he'd had any doubt who'd set him up, he didn't any longer. She'd known she'd be seeing him again.

"I beg your pardon?" she asked haughtily.

He enunciated each word as he stepped toward her. "The woman you hired to steal my camera and laptop? Tell her I want them back along with the photos of your mother and—"

"I have no idea what you're talking about."

He laughed. "Did anyone ever mention that you're a terrible liar?"

She bristled and looked offended. "I don't lie. Nor do I like being accused of something I didn't do."

"Save it," he said before she could deny it again. "I show you a photograph of your mother, and hours later my camera and laptop are stolen and you have no idea what I'm talking about?"

Kat shrugged. "Maybe you should be more careful about who you hang out with." She turned her back to him as she resumed what she'd been doing. Or at least pretended to.

"Look. Someone is going to get a photo of your mother sooner or later. Why go to so much trouble?"

She turned to face him. "Exactly. If not you, then someone else will get her photo. Do you think I really care that you took a photo of my mother with plans to sell it to some sleazy rag? I didn't and I still don't. I've lived in a fishbowl my whole life. I've had people like you in my face with cameras since my father first ran for office. It comes with the territory. My mother is just another casualty."

He took off his hat and scratched the back of his neck as he considered whether or not she was lying. He'd been bluffing earlier. "I'm not buying it. I saw your expression when you recognized your mother in the photograph."

She sighed. "Think what you like."

"Let's talk about another woman, the one you set me up with last night."

Hand on one hip, she turned to study him openly for a moment. "What did this woman look like?"

He described her. "Don't pretend you don't know her."

"I know her *type*." She smiled, noticeably amused. "Come on, weren't you even a little suspicious when she hit on you? She did hit on you, right? That's what I thought, and you fell for it. Whoever set you up must know you."

Max laughed. Kat had lightened up, and he liked her sense of humor. "I'll have you know, women hit on me all the time."

She rolled her eyes. "Chalk this up as a learning experience and move on." She started to turn away again.

"You really don't think I'm going to let you get away with this, do you?"

She sighed and faced him once more. "What option do you have? Even if you had a shred of proof, it would be my word, the daughter of a senator, against your word, a…reporter."

Okay, now she was ticking him off. "I happen to like what I do, and it puts food on my table." He glanced at the photos she was working on. "Who keeps food on your table? I doubt your…hobby of taking pictures is your means of support." He cocked his head at her. "Then again, you don't need to stoop to having a real job, do you?"

KAT HAD KNOWN she would see Max Malone again after he'd ambushed her yesterday. He would want a story about her mother. He would use the photos he'd gotten to bargain with her. This wasn't her first rodeo.

But she hadn't expected him to come in the back way accusing her of stealing his camera and laptop with the photos of her mother. If she'd known how easy it would have been, she might have considered setting him up just for the fun of it, though.

No, she had expected him to come through the front door and make a scene once the gallery opened. She'd been prepared to threaten to call the police on him.

But he'd surprised her in more ways than one. Not many men did that. So she'd let him have his say, waiting to see what his game was. She'd even found the man somewhat amusing at first, but now he was starting to irritate her.

"I'll have you know I take care of myself."

"Is that right? You pay for that fancy SUV you drive?" He laughed. "I didn't think so. Now about my camera—"

"If you think I'm going to replace your camera— What are you doing?" she demanded as he pulled out his cell phone and keyed in three numbers. She'd planned to *threaten* to call the police, but she wouldn't have done it because she didn't want the hassle or the publicity.

"Calling the cops."

"They'll arrest you for breaking into the gallery." She

heard the 911 operator answer. He was calling her bluff. He knew she didn't want the police involved.

"I'd like to report—"

"Fine," she snapped.

He said, "Sorry, my mistake," into the phone and pocketed it again. He eyed her, waiting.

"But I don't have your camera or your laptop."

He studied her for a long moment. "Okay, if you want to play it that way, then what do you have to offer me?" he asked as he leaned against the counter where she'd been working.

She gritted her teeth. Hadn't she suspected that he hadn't really lost his camera or laptop and that he was playing her? She no longer found him amusing. It was time to call a halt to this.

"Even though I had nothing to do with the loss of your camera or laptop, I'll write you a check for new ones just to get rid of you."

He shook his head slowly, his gaze lingering on her long enough that she could feel heat color her cheeks. He made her feel naked, as if he could see her the way no one else could. "*My* camera, *my* laptop, *my* photos. That's the only deal on the table, unless you have something more to offer."

"I just offered you money!"

He shook his head, his gaze warm on her.

She felt her cheeks flush as she realized what he was suggesting. "I have *nothing* more to offer you."

He raised a brow, shoved off the counter and closed the distance between them. "Either I get my camera back, or you're going to have to make it up to me in another way." He was close, too close, but it wasn't fear he evoked. She could smell the scent of freshly showered soap on him. Her gaze went from his blue eyes to his lips and the slight smirk there. The man was so cocky, so arrogant, so sure of the effect he was having on her.

As he brushed his fingertips over her cheek, she felt a tingle before she slapped his hand away. "If you think I'm going to sleep with you—"

"I said something that I would like *better*," he said.

Better than sleeping with her? "You really are a bastard."

He shook his head. "Untrue. Both my parents were married and to each other."

"You're enjoying this."

His smile belied his words. "It's purely business, I assure you. But I appreciate you considering sleeping with me."

She fought the urge to slap his handsome face. "I never—"

"I'm sure you have never," he said. "But we can deal with that later. Right now, I suggest we discuss this over breakfast. I'm starved." He moved away, finally giving her breathing room. "You're buying."

"I don't think so." She was trembling inside, her stomach doing slow somersaults. The man threw her off balance, and he knew it. That made it even worse. She took a couple of deep breaths, shocked that some reporter could get this kind of primitive response from her.

Finally she turned to face him. He was going through her photos with an apparent critical eye. She wanted to grab them from him. The last thing she needed was a critique from him about her art.

"Call the police." She crossed her arms over her chest. "If you think you can blackmail me—"

"These are good, really," he said, turning to look at her as if surprised. "You have a good eye."

She hated how pleased she was, but quickly mentally shook herself. What did he know about photography anyway? Just because he carried around a camera and took underhanded snapshots of people who didn't want their photos taken...

"I'd hoped we could discuss this over pancakes," he said as he stepped away from her photos. "I know something about your mother that you're going to want to hear before you see it in the media."

"There is nothing you can tell me that I would—"

"Your mother isn't just lying about the past twenty-two years. She's been lying since the get-go, and I can prove it." He smiled. "But first I want breakfast. I'm starved."

Don't miss LUCKY SHOT
by B.J. Daniels
available wherever HQN books and
ebooks are sold.

Copyright © 2015 by Barbara Heinlein

COMING NEXT MONTH FROM
⊕ HARLEQUIN®

INTRIGUE

Available December 15, 2015

#1611 REUNION AT CARDWELL RANCH
Cardwell Cousins • by B.J. Daniels
The last of his clan to come home to Big Sky, Montana, Laramie Cardwell wasn't planning to spend the holidays chasing an elusive cat burglar. Now he'll move mountains to capture the mystery woman whose kiss smolders on his lips.

#1612 SMOKY MOUNTAIN SETUP
The Gates: Most Wanted • by Paula Graves
Wrongly accused of murder, FBI agent Cade Landry turns to his former partner—and lover—Olivia Sharp to help him find a killer...and a love that never died.

#1613 SPECIAL FORCES SAVIOR
Omega Sector: Critical Response • by Janie Crouch
To catch terrorists, agent Derek Waterman will need Dr. Molly Humphries, Omega's lead forensic scientist. Working together brings out feelings Derek would rather keep hidden, but when Molly's kidnapped, he will stop at nothing to save her.

#1614 ARRESTING DEVELOPMENTS
Marshland Justice • by Lena Diaz
When he is forced to crash-land his plane in the Everglades, billionaire and former navy pilot Dex Lassiter must partner with Amber Callahan to keep them both from becoming victims of a mysterious killer.

#1615 HUNTER MOON
Apache Protectors • by Jenna Kernan
Apache tracker Clay Cosen's past comes back to haunt him when his ex-love Isabelle Nosie asks him to help clear her name. Clay will need all his skill to ensure her safety—and win her heart.

#1616 TRUSTING A STRANGER • by Melinda Di Lorenzo
Wanted for murder, Graham Calloway has been in hiding for years, until he rescues a beautiful stranger, Keira Niles, from her wrecked car. For the first time he wants a future...but will the killer let him have one?

YOU CAN FIND MORE INFORMATION ON UPCOMING HARLEQUIN® TITLES, FREE EXCERPTS AND MORE AT WWW.HARLEQUIN.COM.

HICNM1215

$7.99 U.S./$9.99 CAN.